Dorothee DeBerry

The RASCAL

Escapades of a Schnauzer named SPORT
Fond Memories

*Bibliographic information published by
German National Library:
The German National Library lists this publication in
the German National Bibliography; detailed bibliographic data are available in the Internet
http://dnb.dnb.de.*

Copyright ©2014 by Dorothee DeBerry
with photos by the author
cover photo by Tita Bayer

Publisher:
BoD – Books on Demand, Norderstedt
ISBN 978-3-7347-4537-9

For George, my dear Husband,
who brought this canine friend
into my life and
let me experience all the joys
that a four-legged companion
could give

Contents

The Vision	**13**
How it came all about	**15**
Gipsy	15
At the Breeder's	20
The Homecoming	**23**
Spoiled? Who?	23
Little Fluff Ball	24
Puppy Looks	25
Getting to know each other	**31**
Housebreaking	31
Burrpp!	33
The Chase	34
Hamburger?	35
Canaries	36
The Intruder	37
Mop, Vacuum Cleaner & Co.	38
Snoopy Snoop	39
Tooth Fairy?	40
Sightseeing Platform	41
Bilingual	42

Dinner Conversation	44
Adventures outside the House	**45**
The Collar	45
The Stairwell	46
Four Legs	47
The Monster	48
Buzzing Vehicles	49
Joggers	50
Romping in the Park	50
Sticks and Balls	53
Lost	55
Trouble in the Park	56
Stone Fences	59
All-Weather-Dog?	60
Riding the Car	65
Bus and Subway Stations	67
Automatic Glass Door	68
SPORT goes Shopping	69
Training	76
Raining on his Parade	79
Bighead	80
Order of Ranks	83
Body Guard	85

Rebellious Times — 93
The Puddle — 93
Yew Bushes — 94
Is he a Rowdy? — 94
The Sandbox — 96
The Trickster — 96
Learning it the hard way — 98

Grooming — 101
Scaled Herring — 104
Second Try — 106
Zombie — 108
Dire Straits — 109
Different kind of Grooming — 112
Is SPORT a Star? — 116

Inter-Canine Relationships — 119
Gipsy — 119
The Irish Wolfhound — 120
The Mongrel — 121
The Shepherd — 123
The SUV — 124

Species of a different Kind — 127
Cats — 127

Horses	**130**
Tasty Creatures!	**131**
Bushy Tails	**133**
Flying Insects	**135**
The Feathered Species	**136**
Man out of Space?	**137**
Neighbors and Visitors	**141**
Teasing Neighbors	**141**
Secret Love	**142**
Workmen	**142**
Unwanted Intruders	**143**
Every Dog's special Friend	**145**
Friends of the House	**147**
Canine Visitors	**151**
Unexpected furry Visitor	**153**
Visiting Other People's House	**157**
Monty's Home	**157**
Charlie's Cat	**158**
At a neigbor's house	**159**
The Home Buddy	**161**
Alone at Home	**161**
Bringing a Surprise	**162**

Imaginary Rabbits	164
Playthings	166
The Pillow	167
Treasure Hunting	168
Where is George?	170
Privacy	171
The Bath Attendant	173
Is SPORT jealous?	174
The Peacemaker	174
The Couch	175
Cuddling Time	177
Jiving	179
Airborne	180
The Big Helper	**185**
Doing the Laundry	185
Sewing Partner	185
The Gardener	187
The Delivery Man	188
SPORT, the Gourmet	**191**
Dog Diet	191
Special Treats	192
The Food Taster	194
Munching Party	195

Weird Tastes	195
Eerie! Eerie!	**197**
Moon Talk	197
Infatuated	198
The Magician	198
Jungles of Madagascar	199
Roots	200
His Health	**203**
Visits to the Vet	203
Difficult Times	**207**
First Signs	207
Did he suffer a Stroke?	209
The Vet Clinic	210
Back with his Pack again	213
Continuing Problems	216
New Vet	217
New Baby in the House?	226
Walking Dispensary	227
SPORT, the Senior	**231**
About the Author	**241**

The Vision

There he was, jumping and racing through the house. Pure joy of life had taken him over. He just had to release his energy, looking for something to get into. He kept us going, more often than not having something mischievous on his mind. Just before, he had nudged George, my dear husband, dropping one of his favorite toys at his feet, in classic play bow pose with front legs down and butt up in the air. Wagging his little stumpy tail, he was bribing George with the most intriguing look in his eyes, smiling "*come on, I want to play tag*". If he put on his charms like this, perhaps accompanied with a slight "*woof*", nobody could withstand this lively little rascal.

George had named him SPORT. He was everything we had visualized, when, some time ago, the idea of getting a dog came up. We had wanted a buddy, a comrade, a road partner and a friend who would be at our side no matter what, going with us through thick and thin, listen attentively when we spoke to him and sense any of our moods, cheering us up and making us laugh with his little antics. One who would be loyal to the end and trust us totally. Who would defend us if someone acted strangely toward us, and who definitely could expect our special care and comfort if he happened to be in need himself. Who would enjoy accompanying us on long walks and entice us to go on a rabbit chase, or run eagerly bringing back a thrown stick, a ball or a chestnut. In short, we envisioned a partner always ready for some action. And that was exactly what SPORT the Schnauzer proved to be – best friend, buddy, and companion – in other words, a true sport.

Now, all you felines out there may hiss at me, this little fellow called SPORT was able to convert me – an avowed cat-enthusiast – into a flying canine-lover. And that came about like this:

How it came all about

Gipsy

Downstairs in our house there was a barbershop. One day, Markus, the owner, decided to have a new dog. And he came home with the sweetest little Schnauzer girl. Gipsy was her name. Her pepper and salt shaded fur was neatly cut, her ears cropped and the tail docked, and her beautiful brownish and slightly sloped eyes were nearly covered by the long curtain of her eyebrows. And, for being a girl, her beard was outstandingly attractive – after all, she was a member of the Schnauzer-family. She was almost grown and a real sophisticated little lady in her posture and behavior.

Gipsy was very shy. She spent many hours of the day in the barbershop, lying in a corner on her cushion, watching customers come and go and probably yearning to be taken for a walk. And that is exactly what happened when George, with his big-hearted self, walked in and took a liking to her. He began to take her out to the park and the green strips in the neighborhood, and she loved it. They made this a habit, and many times early in the morning George went downstairs, picked up Gipsy and took her along on his trip to get his paper and then made a round through the park with her. Almost inevitably, sweet little Gipsy fell in love with him (and that – knowing my husband – was the most logical thing to happen). Soon, about every morning at the same time, she began to sit quietly at the front entrance of the house or – if the front door happened to be open – she would sit there right in front of our apartment door on the first floor upstairs, patiently waiting for George to appear.

This went on for a while. Then, one day, George began to talk about having his own dog. He was hearing me out what I would think about it. After all, since I was leaning more toward the members of the feline family, we had been kidding each other constantly about who would be smarter or make more fun, a cat or a dog. I knew cats very well, always having had some around when I was growing up in the country. I had observed their playing and hunting rituals, seen them depleting the mouse population and occasionally bringing home a rabbit or a blackbird. I had watched their hilarious attempts to catch a squirrel, chasing it up a tree, where the squirrel – scoffing and loudly chattering – waited for the cat to climb up just close enough before it, the squirrel, simply jumped gracefully from one treetop to the next, while the cat had difficulties to back down the stem again and try another assault up the next tree, only to fail anew, accompanied by some more ridicule of the intended prey.

Cats had really grown to my heart when I watched them raise and teach their own kittens and being smart, intriguing or just catty, and of course – best of all – had experienced their cuddling and smooching, their purring tenderness. Could a dog ever be like that?

I had seen some dogs in my childhood neighborhood. Fifi the Spitz for instance, a white unpleasant and constantly barking nuisance. Or the big red-haired Chowchow, who suspiciously watched the front yard of his owner where my mother always sent me to fetch some fresh cow's milk. One day I came back home without the milk, being ashamed and therefore lied to my mother that the milk had been sold out, while in reality I had just been too darn scared to pass by this growling monster.

And then there was Hugo the dachshund. He lived around the corner at the end of the dirt road leading away from our house and that of another neighbor. Hugo was not exactly the smartest of all dogs, but at least he was not mean. As a matter of fact, everyone thought that he was a masochist. Every day he came strolling harmlessly down this dirt road to pay the two houses at our end a visit. And every day Peter, the neighbor's big black and white tomcat, was hiding maliciously behind the corner of the house next to ours, kneading his feet impatiently and stooping his back, waiting for

Hugo's nose to appear at the curve right in front of him. Irresistible opportunity for Peter, who jumped on a shocked Hugo, hissing, slapping and scratching him while the poor victim tried to escape, howling and hobbling as fast and far away as his short dachshund legs would take him, tail way under his belly. It was clear, this was cat's territory! But nevertheless, the next day Hugo showed up again….same procedure as always.

These episodes did not exactly have me develop an emotional line to dogs, I did not care much, they were neutral to me. As I had never had a dog of my own, and actually was nipped by a jealous German Shepherd when I was a child, it was kind of hard to convince me of the joys of having a canine companion.

But then again, I must admit, aside from the above insignificant events, I have always loved most animals. And now, where George was talking my ears off trying to persuade me to get our own dog, I melted and became confident that a dog and I could become friends as well. A very important part was that we would have enough time to care for a dog and give him all the devotion that he needed. As George was already retired – he had spent his working life in the Air Force – the time factor proved to be no problem. So we became all open to add a four-legged friend to our household.

But what kind of dog should it be? Should it be a male or a female? Both having their advantages and disadvantages, the female perhaps being more soft and subtle while a male could be more hardheaded. Should we get a purebred or rather a mixed breed? We would love either one. Should we go to a breeder or check out the animal shelters? Going to the latter would probably make us come home with half a dozen lonely souls.

We were undecided, especially as we really had a puppy in mind that we could raise and mold ourselves. We wanted a dog not too small and not a constant barker and actually fancied the bigger kind, like a German Shepherd for instance, who is known for his intelligence, devotion and nobility. Or perhaps a Labrador, also said to be intelligent as well as high-spirited, good-natured and playful? What about a Golden Retriever, the animated sunbeam with his open, lovely and friendly facial expression that automatically makes you smile back at him? Maybe one of those healthy, bold and energetic bundles of muscles, a Giant Schnauzer, who is also known to be intelligent, absolutely loyal, sensitive and playful? Or rather a mix of some of these?

Our fantasy was acting up. But then we thought about the space these dogs need. Our medium-sized city apartment definitely would not have done them right. And besides, as I did not have any special experience with dogs, the larger breeds might have been too difficult for me to handle – butter-hearted as I am.

We came to the conclusion that fitting best to our situation and us would be a frisky, bright, family-friendly and medium-sized dog that could tolerate city apartment life. One perhaps like Gipsy? Yes, why did we not think about that right away! And in addition, Markus had just come up with the news about a breeder, whose dog – a Standard Schnauzer – had recently given birth to a litter of eleven puppies. With shiny eyes, George and I looked at each other, the decision was made, it was going to be a Schnauzer. Sweet little Gipsy had convinced us.

At the Breeder's

So one sunny morning, Markus took George out to this particular breeder. Meanwhile, staying home and waiting for George to come back with some news, my imagination was running wild. Just think about it, a basket full of squirmy, frisky, little, rubber-boned, fuzzy and cuddly Schnauzer puppies! My heart jumped! Yes, I really liked the idea now of having a little puppy around, keeping us company. George was quite excited too. The puppies George went to see were still too small, though, about five weeks old, and we were to wait until they had grown to be eight weeks. However, George had already made up his mind and picked the one he wanted. When the breeder let Markus and George take a look at the puppies, some of them became timid and tried to waddle away. George had bent down, holding out his hand to let them get a sniff of it. And there, one daring little fellow took all his heart, walked up to this strange hand, let out a deep warning growl that would have made a Doberman Pinscher proud and bit boldly into poor George's finger. *Ouch*! This fresh little handful of a would-be-Schnauzer did not only leave a bleeding imprint on George's finger, but also a lasting impression on his future owner, who couldn't help it but smile and gently rub the back of this spunky little rascal. Yes, this was the one! This was going to be SPORT! A small portion of his fur was cut so as to mark him for identification later when he was to be picked up and taken to his new home.

The Homecoming

Spoiled? Who?

Time went by. We eagerly looked forward to picking up SPORT and bringing him home. The coming weekend was planned for this event. We had everything prepared to make him feel comfortable. He would find his own and very personal doghouse in one room. It even had his name written above the entrance: "Gallo von Biedrich", his name according to his birth certificate. But this was only the official name, he would be called "SPORT", the name that George had picked and which turned out to really match his personality.

Beside his doghouse, a cushioned basket – his "nest" for daytime leisure – was placed in another room, and – we did not know it at that time – later on in addition he would adopt and fiercely defend a couch in a third room as being his personal property. He had his own towels with the imprint of a "Snoopy"-image. And a special corner in the kitchen was reserved for all his snacks, goodies or rewards and everything else a happy dog might need. Yes, and several squeaky and fluffy toys were also waiting for him. Boy, this dog was already spoiled before he arrived! Or was he? No, I believe these were the bare necessities and basics that every dog should expect and be entitled to in a new home.

Little Fluff Ball

The week before we were supposed to pick him up, I was coming home from work and – while opening the door – I saw a little fluff ball sitting in the kitchen corner on a towel. He stared at me, ready to take off. I stared at him. What was this…? This must be…. yes, this was SPORT! *"Well, George, you gooney goo-goo, you couldn't wait and went out all alone and got him earlier!"* Oh, was this little fellow cute! I bent down. He eased away. I spoke softly to him. I did not want to scare him. To him I must have seemed a giant monster in a still strange surrounding, a monster that he had never seen before, and he did not know how it might act. But this monster obviously was friendly, bending down and carefully holding out a hand for him to sniff at. Slowly and cautiously, SPORT made a few wobbly steps toward me, not leaving an eye off of me. He was so adorable, I had to hold myself back not to grab and hug him. But that would have been too early. I had to give him time to adjust to this new situation. Ever so softly, his black shiny puppy nose touched my hand and – surprise – nothing bad happened to him! He looked at me, wondering. I looked at him, also wondering. I had to smile –

and it seemed as if he was doing the same. A long and intense friendship had begun!

That same evening we all took it somewhat easy with each other. SPORT had not taken his first car ride so well. He had become sick on the way to his new home and seemed to be feeling a bit under the weather. We were around, but we did not bother him much, while he snooped around a little bit and then settled down in his doghouse, which he took over as his personal property right away. The next day he was all right again, although he looked as if he was missing his mama and siblings. But then, after a day or two, he seemed to have adjusted and began to investigate his new surroundings.

Puppy Looks

Of course, every dog owner believes that his new puppy is the sweetest, cutest and smartest of all. So did I, even more so. I just have to exaggerate now, because – having always been a serious cat admirer – I did not have the faintest idea how quickly this little fellow would work himself right into my heart and make me understand what "happiness is having a puppy" is really all about. SPORT was a true enrichment to our lives. And yes, he WAS the cutest thing one could imagine. Still tiny, but full of spunk.

He had these giant paws and clumsy rubber-boned movements that you see only in very young dogs. The way he sat down was also typical for a puppy his age. Resting on his rump, he

stretched his seemingly boneless hind legs forward, having them reach in a slight V-shape almost up to his front legs, which supported his upright posture, while having his still pinkish little round belly sticking out.

His head was rather big compared to the rest of his body, causing him to get his first nickname: Bighead. This indicated not only the size of his head, but in fact also the strong will he was to develop on his way to adulthood.

Still wrapped in his puppy wool, his fur was shiny, soft and cuddly, while over time it was to become sort of coarse and bristly. The color was pepper and salt, still somewhat on the dark side with slightly lighter areas at the tip of his nozzle and eyebrows. His paws also had a lighter shade than the rest of his fur, which made them seem to be even bigger than they were in reality. And when SPORT turned around, his little meager butt looked as if he had been sitting on a dusty flour bag.

In contrast to his tail, which had been docked to a mere one and a half inches, his ears had been left natural, and at his tender age of almost eight weeks, SPORT was not able yet to make them stand up and move them around. Their V-shaped body was flapping down forward at the sides of his head, giving him this innocent and harmless look. But don't be fooled, he was a real mischievous character and we learned very quickly –

after he finally mastered to twist his ears around, giving him all these different facial expressions – when he was up to something. Yes, SPORT could talk with his ears!

And then there were his teeth, – milk teeth, yes, but oh boy – pointed and razor-sharp like a shark's teeth. After playing and roughhousing with him, one could look as having been in a fuzz-tearing catfight. We could not bite him back the way as his siblings might have done, meaning

that they would playfully teach each other that teeth can hurt and having them develop a sense for their own strength. Therefore SPORT had to listen to a lot of *"ooohs!"* and *"outchs!"* and *"no-Sport-cut-that-outs!"* before he understood not to bite.

At this young stage of his life, SPORT's face displayed only a clue yet of the arched eyebrows and long mustache and whiskers, which make an adult Schnauzer so distinct. Only a few stubbles hinted toward the beautiful long beard to grow later, giving him this proud and sophisticated Schnauzer-appearance. His eyebrows were still short, not yet falling over his eyes. And he was growing these unbelievably long lashes which were later to keep the then full eyebrows from dropping too closely over his face.

His bright and very alert eyes were brownish and slightly sloped, and he could look at you so intensely that you had to wonder what was going on in his mind. Perhaps he was just a human in a dog's suit? A sentence I had read somewhere before popped up in my head, where Schnauzers were described as being the dogs with a human brain. Well, we were about to learn how much truth there was in this.

Getting to know each other

Housebreaking

The following time was one of getting to know each other. In order for SPORT not to feel lonely or scared in his new home, especially at night, we had set up his doghouse in our bedroom, where he had our company and we could hear every whimper he made. We became totally focused on him. Every little sound or move our new friend made, had us waking up.

Although his dog mammy had already trained him well enough that he would not soil his own bedding, he still happened to have an accident around the house every now and then. So we tried to watch him closely in order to stop him in time and take him downstairs immediately. For the same reason, we put a gate on his hut and closed it at night. So, whenever he was ready to wee-wee, he started to whine and wanted out. George, the good soul, meticulously took over the responsibility of carrying our new friend downstairs every second or third hour, around the clock, and put him under a nearby tree. SPORT understood very fast where to do his business, and there were no problems any more in his new home. Very soon the gate was removed from his hut also at night and he could roam around freely in the whole house.

There was a short fallback though. As we had barred SPORT from the living room area during the first weeks or so for the reasons given above, he promptly had a mishap right there when he was finally allowed in. What was going on – why did this happen? SPORT was still too small to intentionally mark a new territory this way. He surely did not even know at this young age what marking a territory was, not to mention the technique on how to do this, as will be described later. But then something dawned on us. He had already learned that the space around his bedding and adjacent living area in the house was not to be soiled. But because the living room was still strange to him, he may have looked at it as not being his immediate and standard living zone. Could it be that SPORT's first impression was *"mmmh, sure doesn't look or smell familiar here, nice room though – but what the heck, I have to wee-wee..."* and there came the waterfall? If that was the case, we had to change our attitude. We tried it, although it took us a bit of effort to let SPORT also roam around the living room from now on despite his occasional unappreciated action in there. But we hoped that he would stop this as soon as he looked upon this room as also being part of his usual and permanent territory in the house, meaning that it was a no-no to make a mess there.

And it worked. Not long after his first incident, SPORT gave up any ambition in this respect. Anyway, just as well as we began to understand the miraculous thinking process of our dog, he also grasped very quickly the overall rules of what was allowed in the house and what should rather be done outside, and soon this whole matter was no theme any more.

Burrpp!

It was real fun and a great experience to watch SPORT developing. One of his greatest joys was – naturally – to eat. While his dish was being prepared, he didn't leave an eye off his master. Sitting on his tiny butt, he would squirm impatiently, moving his front feet to and forth, the tip of his little pink tongue moving in and out of his watery mouth "*hurry up, hurry up*", and – in his excitement – he produced these gentle, rolling and anticipating sounds. Then, when he was finally munching away, he growled "*Grrrrr!*" at anybody daring to pass by too close. "*SPORT, don't talk with a full mouth*!" However, in time he understood that we were not – like his siblings – trying to compete for his food. After he was finished, he would turn around, lick his chops, then take a slurp of water, walk away and – very self-contentedly – belch like a Great Dane. "*Burrpp!*" He was a real character!

The Chase

Coming home from work in the evenings, I usually reserved the first hour or so for SPORT. George didn't mind as he had had him already all day. SPORT used to come running to the door, look me up and down, jump around my feet, his little stumpy tail going like a windmill. I greeted him with a "scritch" on his chops, and then off he was, racing into the living room, "*tag me, tag me*", stopping and turning around looking to make sure that I was following him. And the chase could begin.

He loved being chased around in the house. He was wild, he would jump up on the couch, fly across the lower table, race into the bedroom, take a leap up on the bed and turn around in mid-air to see if the chase was still on. In his excitement he used to smack his front legs as if to take off, just waiting for you to come close enough. He always managed to find a way to tease you about which direction he was going and then slip by and zip back into the other room. When he eventually became tired, he slumped down on the couch or simply on the floor, out of breath, but happy-faced.

That was the time to cuddle. I used to hold him and rub him all over. He could never get enough of this, loved being crawled behind his ears. He would lick my hands and then roll over on his side or his back, letting me rub his little round tummy. There I sometimes came across his funny spot and he would toss about with one of his hind legs. These were happy moments where I could not resist smooching him behind his ears – mmmmh, this little puppy smelled so good! After such an affectionate pause, SPORT kept lying there for a while, being content and anticipating the moment. But just as often he would get up, walk into the kitchen, take a slurp of water, and get ready for another round of romping.

Hamburger?

We were curious as to how SPORT would react to the first toy that we presented to him. It was a soft rubber chew toy, shaped like a real-life juicy hamburger. We were sure, SPORT didn't care much about the looks of it. But it rolled around so enticingly! This looked like fun! He jumped on it. Eeeek, it squeaked! It seemed to be alive! He jumped back, looking at us, being puzzled. We rubbed the hamburger lightly with our finger. SPORT watched carefully, but nothing bad happened. So he cautiously sneaked up on this strange thing, touched it with his paw, jumping back again, just in case. Yes, it did squeak again, and at the same time it tumbled over from the clumsy tap SPORT had given it. Now he became really curious. He had to investigate this more closely. He sniffed at it, it didn't seem to bite! He tapped it again, chasing it while it rolled away. Picking it up, chewing it, making it squeak some more, throwing it high into the air, catching it, rolling around on the floor with it – SPORT was having fun!

Canaries

One of my colleagues had given me a tube of tennis balls for SPORT to play with. And did he play with them! Not only the yellow balls got his fancy, also the tube itself. I used to hold the tube sideways so that the balls would slowly drop out of it, bouncing onto the floor, where they were being received, jumped on, chased and collected again by an enthused SPORT. Then I made the tube crackle. At first, this sound intimidated him, but later this became part of the ritual and he included it in our game. SPORT seldom played with just one single tennis ball alone. He tried to chase and fetch all of them at the same time, as good as that would work. He usually couldn't make up his mind which one to follow first. He would catch and hold one of the balls in his mouth while following the other ones bouncing and rolling around. But when he reached for them he could not really grab any because he had his mouth already full with his first fetch, or he would lose this one again. But eventually, he managed to gather them all together, then lie down, holding the balls in a row between his front paws, sometimes smacking and pinching them, rearranging and pushing them around with his nose, acting like he was watching over a flock of yellow birds. That's why we called this the "canary" game.

The Intruder

One day, we heard some strange noises coming from the other room. We checked and saw SPORT parading in front of the mirror. He had detected another dog in the house! Growling and making his hair stand up, he tried to look bigger and impress the supposed intruder. But what was that? Just when he snarled at him *"grrrrrh, get lost!"*, the other one fluffed up as well and dared to grumble back at him. And while SPORT moved aggressively toward him, the stranger imitated this too! SPORT was not going to tolerate this! *"Bark, bark, bark!"* They stood nose to nose. Eeeek! This was cold! SPORT jumped back. So did the intruder. Was he perhaps afraid? This was his chance. SPORT decided to finally chase this sucker off. He snarled and again moved back toward him. But so did the intruder. SPORT was bewildered. Something was wrong! He looked at us, question marks in his eyes. We placed ourselves behind him, so that he could see our images in the mirror too. But this seemed to confuse him even more. We petted him and rubbed his head, gestured toward him in the mirror. He turned around, looked at us, then again looked into the mirror. And slowly, slowly it seemed to dawn on him who that was in the mirror. But it took a few more sessions until he realized that this stranger in the mirror did not deserve any of this adverse attention. As a matter of fact, many times later we caught him just standing in front of the mirror, admiring his image. Was he aware that he was looking at himself? Was he perhaps vain? It amused us to watch him this way.

Mop, Vacuum Cleaner & Co.

SPORT had another "enemy" in the house. Our green mop. As soon as the mop was being used, SPORT barked and barked, jumped on it, pulling and shaking it. There was no chance of using it as long as he was around. He seemed to have immense fun doing this and then stand back, grinning from one ear to the other, as if to say *"great job, eh?"* Whatever drove him to this behavior, he never gave that up. He sometimes even barked at the closet where he knew that we used to store the mop: *"Bark, bark, come on out of there, come on out...!"*

It was a different story with the vacuum cleaner. SPORT seemed to have tremendous respect for it. In the beginning he angrily barked at this loudly humming beast, but stayed out of its way, carefully stepping back if it moved too close to him. Mostly though, he preferred to just leave the room.

He wouldn't leave the room but suspiciously followed the broom sweeping to and forth, being undecided whether to snap and bite at it or rather leave it alone. If the broom turned toward him, he backed off, but immediately trailed it again when it moved on. He seemed to be sure that one day he would find out what made it tick and then he could scare it off!

SPORT evidently thought that mop, vacuum cleaner and broom were living creatures invading his territory and had to be watched carefully.

Snoopy Snoop

"Sport, what's wrong!" I almost shouted. He was strolling around with a dark rusty-red nose. It looked like blood. *"Come here, little fellow, what happened?"* SPORT walked over to me, all calm, looking at me with big innocent eyes, wondering what I was so upset about. I dabbed his nose with a tissue, it also became dark red, yet it did not seem to be blood, it was some kind of dry sub-

stance. I was relieved. But what could it be? I looked around. There were several marks of the same color where SPORT must have touched his nose walking around, at the lower end of a table cloth, on the side of the living room couch. I was at a loss, what was it? And then I detected it. Following the trail of rusty-red specks, my eyes fell on a bouquet of flowers being placed on our lower table near the couch. Among these flowers were a few lilies, widely opened up, showing their dark red pollen. That's what it was! I had seen SPORT sniffing curiously at other blossoms before, so he must have stuck his nose right into these lilies, getting it colored this way. *"SPORT, you scared me to death."* I was glad that the fuzz was all about nothing. I cleaned up SPORT's nose and moved the lilies to a higher place where SPORT could not reach them. In the future I would be more careful what to put where, as SPORT loved to stick his nose into every bunch of flowers or to every bowl with fruits that I placed on this low table

Tooth Fairy?

One day I was walking around the house barefooted. *Ouch!* What was that? I had stepped on something and hurt my foot. Hopping on one foot, holding the other, I looked around to see what had caused this pain. And there he was, standing behind me with a mischievous look on his face, grinning from one ear to the other, flashing a giant gap in his row of baby teeth! Well, would you have known, dogs change their teeth too! SPORT was shedding his milk teeth and I had stepped on one! The following days, we found more of these razor-sharp little things. We saved them all – who knows, maybe there is a tooth fairy after all? Good thing about his second set of teeth was, they were not as sharp as in his first set and you could wrestle with him now without getting marked all over.

Sightseeing Platform

SPORT was very curious. Being in the house, he wondered what all that noise was coming from the street through the window. He wanted to see. He jumped up on the couch nearby, climbed onto the back and from there tried to reach the windowsill. But the distance was a bit too far for him, his body was still too short. He kept trying, squirming, peeping, running to us for help, jumping back up on the couch, showing us what he wanted. So we usually opened one window, picked up SPORT and placed him right there in the open window, holding him tightly. He would sit down, pressing his back against us for support, very confident that he was securely protected from falling. He was not the least bit afraid of the height. He curiously watched everything that was going on outside. Often people would look up, smile and sometimes speak to a gleaming SPORT, who enjoyed this attention immensely. When after a while he had enough, he pushed back, letting us know that he wanted to go back inside. Putting him down on the floor, I usually told him *"go to George and tell him that you have been in the window."* And SPORT would run over to George, jumping around with a happy face, stumpy tail twirling and telling in so many ways about his adventure in the window. George was showing his delight, having SPORT proudly strutting around. I believe it began here that SPORT developed his special way of communicating with us, something that really fascinated us about him.

Bilingual

When George or I talked to SPORT, he grasped quickly what the meaning of many words and phrases were, especially when they meant something pleasant for him. As George and I were two different nationalities, people used to ask us in what language we would communicate with SPORT. It was funny, George, the American, spoke German to the dog, I, the German, spoke English to him. We used to joke about the fact that SPORT actually was bilingual. But then again, many phrases sound very similar in English and German, like *"come here"* and *"komm her"* or *"sit"* and *"sitz"*. SPORT also grasped the meaning of some longer phrases, in both languages. Whether we said *"Geh in dein Bett"* or *"Go to your bed"*, SPORT would turn around immediately – ears down though – and walk to his room and get on his bunk - almost like a robot under remote control. We could get him from any corner in the house when we asked *"gehen wir spazieren?"* or *"are we going for a walk?"* Then SPORT came racing from where ever he had just been, jumping around happily and eagerly waiting for us to put his collar on. While I sat there, tying up my shoes, SPORT stood across from me, trying to hypnotize me to hurry up, his quick-witted eyes following every move I made. Sometimes I asked him *"gibst du mir ein Bussi?"*, meaning *"will you give me a smooch?"* Then he looked at me with big eyes, thinking for a moment, and then all of a sudden he would rush forward and plant a dog-kiss right on my eye or wherever he could just land it.

We realized that SPORT could understand more than we had given him credit for. When we resorted to saying *"Schweineohr"* instead of *"pig ear"*, or *"Leckerli"* instead of *"goody"*, he quickly grasped that the two different words meant the very same tasty thing. And his ears went straight up and he excitedly jumped on his feet, expecting a treat for his taste buds. So if the occasion asked for it, we started – just imagine – spelling some of the words so he would not understand them and have expectations that we were not going to fill all the time.

Dinner Conversation

Sometimes, when we sat at the table in the evening having dinner, SPORT placed himself on one of his favorite spots, way up on the top back of the couch across from the dinner table, following every word of our conversation. Being very alert, he moved his head from one side to the other, looking at whoever was just speaking. And then he would butt in, starting some kind of sing-sang, going up and down the gamut, looking real earnest. If one of us said something, SPORT would follow that with his singing murmur. We are sure that he believed that he was really talking. It was okay when we responded like *"Yes, isn't that right, Sport? We totally agree with you."* But if we waited too long addressing him, his voice went up and he would put a little more pressure behind his "conversation" until we replied with something like *"Aw, come on, Big-head, are you sure of that? Prove it!"* Lying there like a Sphinx, face real serious, his stumpy tail began to move and he now and then would slam one of his paws forward as if to underline his point. SPORT was a lot of fun having around. All three of us really enjoyed being with each other.

Adventures outside the House

The Collar

As we were going outside with SPORT for his walks, he had to get used to wearing a collar and a leash. And as dogs usually do not like to be on a leash, we decided to trick him a little bit and make it look like a fun game for him. We had bought him a little yellowish leather collar, studded with a row of metal rivets. Being suspicious, he first sniffed at it, then took it into his mouth. What was this strange thing? A toy? *"No, SPORT, this is not a toy, but you may just as well drag it through the house because it is yours."* "*Oh, how nice of you! Come on collar*" and he dragged it around. Sometimes we playfully laid it on top of him. Then he would pull it down, shaking it wildly. But after a while he seemed to become more familiar with it and he did not mind when we draped it around his neck, leaving it there for a short period of time. And eventually, he accepted collar and leash to be part of his life, after all, it meant that he was going out for a walk, which he loved most of all.

The Stairwell

The first few months that SPORT was living with us, he was still too small to walk up or down the stairs. As his bones and joints were not fully developed yet, we did not want to take the risk of them becoming damaged from the strain of climbing these high stairs. So we carried him both up and downstairs. This seemed to be the most natural thing for SPORT to happen. He would walk to the side of the door, put himself into position to be picked up, and then, resting comfortably in our arms, he looked around, head high up, probably feeling like a king reigning from a sedan-chair.

But the day of rude awakening was coming fast. After several months of developing from a wobbly puppy into a much stronger youth, he had to face reality. When we did not pick him up for the first time, but instead kept proceeding downstairs, encouraging him to follow us, he protested. *"Peep, peeeep! What are you doing? Don't leave me behind!"* He was walking to and forth at the top of the stairs, but did not dare trying to go down a step all by himself. *"Peep, peep!"* He was in agony. *"Peeeep!"*

We held out a hand to support him. *"Come on SPORT, you can do it."* He pushed himself against the hand for balance, still being reluctant.

Very carefully he reached down to the next step with one of his front paws, leaning heavily against our hand, followed by the other feet, one after the other, still being quite uneasy because of the height of the stairs. But then he did it! He had mastered his first step of the stairs! *"Hey, we knew it, you are a brave little fellow! You did it! Now you come and handle the rest of it!"* Slowly, step by step, supported by hand and encouraged by words, he finally conquered this hurdle to the outside world. And before long, he was racing down the stairs like it was nothing and as if he had never been doing anything else.

Four Legs

SPORT – as most dogs do – loved the outside. He was a great buddy and a lot of fun to be with. Being a puppy, he had yet to learn a lot about the wonders of this world. When he saw all these other dogs lifting a leg every now and then, he did not understand. He stared at them being puzzled. "*Crazy world! Legs are for walking, not for lifting up!*" he seemed to be thinking. Naturally he wanted to know what that was all about. In the beginning, he used to walk up to the dog in process, looking and sniffing curiously – and sometimes even getting his nose wet this way. *"Goodness, SPORT, you really don't know about that yet?"* He kept trying to imitate what he saw, but it did not work out so easily. And then I missed the great day! George came home laughing, *"Guess what he did today. He finally managed to lift his leg."* George described what had happened. SPORT needed to wee-wee, positioned himself near a pole and probed to lift a leg. But it was the wrong one, he couldn't keep the balance and then tumbled over. He got up and gave George, who was trying not to chuckle too obviously, an embarrassed look, *"Don't you laugh at me, you got only two legs, but I have to deal with four!"* During the same outing, though, he finally got it together, he had learned which leg on which side to lift depending on the edge he was standing to the object he was going to baptize. SPORT had mastered another milestone on his way to adulthood.

The Monster

One evening, it was already dark, George and I were just coming home from a walk together with SPORT and were crossing over to this sidewalk in the neighborhood, when tiny little SPORT began to growl. He had seen something that was suspicious to him. He ran forward and started to bark, loud and aggressively. As we came closer, SPORT turned around looking at us, then looking again at the object that had raised his hostility. *"Bark, bark, there is a big monster, tell it to get out of the way. It is blocking us off! Bark, bark!"* *"But, SPORT, this is just a dumb chair that somebody had put out on the sidewalk to be taken to the dumpsite."* This answer did not impress him at all. He simply refused to pass by this old chair. He was not afraid, but it annoyed him badly. And while we finally managed to lure him around it, he was still barking and fussing. Even after being on the other side walking away, he would turn around again and motion back toward this object, standing there with a reproachful expression on his face and complaining some more, hair all fluffed up. He felt really provoked. We were sure that he was going to dream about chasing some monsters that night.

Buzzing Vehicles

SPORT did not care much about a kid zipping by on a skateboard. That left him cold. But if a motorcycle dared to buzz along, he exploded into a hysterical fireball, chasing after this loud noise-making vehicle, barking at the top of his lungs. I almost had a heart attack when I saw him doing this the first time. This was simply too dangerous. We had to get serious with this spry and daring little monster and teach him how to get his temper under control. Not an easy task, but George, with a lot of patience, repetition and sometimes-necessary tough love, managed to train our dog to become a well-behaved and dependable partner over time.

Joggers

SPORT had a different thing about joggers. He would not chase them or try to bite their heels. That we would not have allowed. But he still ran and caught up with them, running alongside in a kind of cadence march, trying to imitate their step. At the same time, he kept looking the jogger up and down, having this expression on his face as if to say *"what is this silly thing you are doing, why can't you walk like any normal person?"* This almost without fail made the jogger get out of rhythm, then chuckle, and look around for the owner to keep this impertinent canine away from him. It was sometimes hard to call SPORT to order, because what we thought to be funny was not always funny to the other party.

Romping in the Park

We liked to take SPORT to the big park where he could run around freely and play on the grass and meet all the other dogs. As a Puppy, he would race ahead, *"yap, yap, yap"*, then slide along in the clover with his nose down, butt in the air, rolling around on the green and *"sniff, sniff, sniff."* He loved the scent of clover.

And there were all the other four-legged friends of two-legged owners. He had to meet them all. *"Sniff, sniff."* Most of them were friendly, some of them were disinterested – SPORT, being so young, did not yet have his distinctive male adult smell and, therefore, not being a sparring partner or sex object. He did not quite understand that, he tried so hard to get their attention. But then there were so many other dogs that wanted to play also.

SPORT was in his element, he was cheerfully running and romping around, his high-pitched puppy-voice yapping with joy among all the other commotion that was going on. If he got tired, he would come back to us, panting and happy-faced, rest a while, getting a few stroking units, and then go on having a good time again.

There was a water faucet at some point in the park. Whenever we passed by there, we would draw him a bowl of fresh water, and away he slurped. *"Slurp, slurp, slurp."* This park was his extended living room. Whenever we had made a round or two through this rather large park and George or I were ready to go back home, SPORT wanted to make another round. This little fellow kept us on our feet, fit and in form.

Sticks and Balls

If SPORT happened to find a stick, he would grab it and proudly carry it around, *"look what I got!"* One day, he found this very thin and long twig. He grabbed it very strategically right in the middle. And, while running with his head high in the air, he tried to balance this remarkably long twig carefully so that it would not tip over at the ends. This was not easy for him to do and he was so absorbed in this delightful task that he did not realize that he was blocking off every pedestrian who wanted to walk past him. The twig reached all across the walkway. Most people smiled tolerantly at this, understanding SPORT being so proud of his find. But we still had to put a stop to this and therefore playfully got his attention on something else so he would drop and leave the stick behind.

At other times, he used to nudge us to make sure that we realized the new treasure he had just found and then go chase him for it. If we were able to get it, we had to throw it for him to fetch and bring it back. But nobody was to really take it away from him. Oh no! He wanted to carry home everything. This was hard work for him, because sometimes his eyes were bigger than his mouth or endurance. If the stick was not just a twig, but a full-fledged tree branch – yes, the bigger, the better – then he could only carry or drag it but so far, then he would have to drop and leave it. At those times we were lucky. At other times, he insisted to take the stick or whatever it was into the house and hide it. We usually discarded of it when he was not around to complain. He would never search for any of it later anyway. But some items he was dead serious about.

One day he found this soccer ball under a bush, he could hardly open his mouth wide enough to grab it. But somehow he managed to hold it. *"No, you are not going to take it away from me,"* SPORT growled, *"this one I am going to die for."* At least that's what George explained to me, when both of them walked into the house with this smudgy ball. SPORT took it right away into his doghouse, where he knew we would not bother him. There he worked on it – *"yes, it's mine, its mine"* – and tried to chew on it until we heard this sound, *pffffhhhh!* Well, he had finally managed to ruin the ball by punching a hole into it with his sharp teeth. But that didn't matter to him, now he could grab and hold it much better when we were wrestling for it. This ball was one of his most cherished treasures which he always defended as being his and only his. If we had let him have his way all the time, he would have carried home half of the park

Lost

One day in the park, we tried to find out what he would do if we accidentally lost each other. We were hiding behind a big tree, peeking carefully around the corner to see how he would act. SPORT was puzzled, walking a few steps in different directions, carefully looking around to find us. Then he didn't hesitate too long, he ran straight toward the exit of the park where he knew our car was parked. We were relieved when we realized that he would not panic too easily and we got out from behind the tree, calling his attention. Happily he raced toward us, and we hugged and praised him, having a bit of a bad conscious because we had put him into this situation.

Then, one evening, I was walking him, unsuspectingly. Everything was peaceful and quiet. Quiet? Too quiet it appeared to me after a while. Where was my dog? He seemed to have disappeared! I called him – no response. I looked around – no SPORT anywhere. *"SPORT?"* Silence. Fear crept up in me. What if somebody had grabbed and kidnapped him? *"SPORT?!"* An unbearable artificial silence was in the air. But there, what was that? My eyes caught a faint shadow – this little charlatan was standing there real still and motionless half under a group of bushes – trying to hide. Well, turn-about is fair play, isn't it! As the color of SPORT's coat was pepper and salt, this gave him a sort of camouflage, which made it hard to detect him at dawn. And evidently he knew that. *"Well, look who is there!"* I called on him. *"I can see you, I can see you"*, I ran toward him. Now he came out of his hideout, mischievous grin on his face, his little stumpy-tail was wagging. He had done it again! I grabbed and hugged him, *"You little rascal, you really got me worried."* It was everything but boring taking him for a walk!

Trouble in the Park

SPORT was very attached to George and me. Even though we took him along whenever we could and had him exposed to many different situations and people, he hesitated to listen to or follow anyone but us. However, this one day, Markus, who was about to take Gipsy to the park, thought it would be a good idea to take SPORT along. Now, as SPORT had never been taken out by anyone but George or me, he naturally was somewhat reluctant to go with Markus although he knew him from being around all the time. At first he ran right beside of him, believing that we would be following them. When he realized that we were going to stay behind, he immediately came back, looking at us with question marks all over his face. *"It's okay, Sport, you can go with Markus"*, we encouraged him. *"We will be here when you come back again. Look, Gipsy is going too. Go on, it's all right."* Hesitantly, SPORT walked again toward Markus, turning around to give us some doubtful looks. But when Gipsy jumped into the car, which was to take them to the park, SPORT followed her. And off they went.

It was a strange feeling. We had given SPORT into the hands of someone else for the first time to take care of him while we were not around. We wondered how he was going to handle this. However, we were kind of nervous. SPORT was so focused on us – what if something happened and we were not there to be at his side? I guess we were just too protective. We had to let go. SPORT was a smart fellow, he knew what to do in situations and we were sure that he also knew to find his way home alone if necessary. Besides, we trusted Markus and his abilities with dogs, he had done a great job with Gipsy.

But time went by, it was too long for just a regular outing in the park. They had not come back yet. Were we too nervous? We waited a bit longer, but then decided to drive over to the park ourselves to see what was going on. By the time we got downstairs, however, Markus' car had just arrived. Markus opened the door and SPORT raced toward us, greeting us happily. *"Man, that dog of yours is really difficult to handle"*, Markus claimed. *"When we were ready to go home, he would just not go back into the car again. I tried to lure him, I tried to grab him, I shouted at him, nothing worked!"* What had happened? Of course, SPORT could not express what had caused him to be so uncooperative, but he must have had a reason. Surely, he did not respect Markus as his alpha-person, or he would have listened to him. Markus said that everything went on normal, they did their walk, but when he was ready to leave, SPORT would not come and go back into the car again as he was told to do. After trying over and over and being unsuccessful, Markus had become so frustrated that he was about to leave SPORT behind and call on us for support. But at last, with the help of Gipsy, who jumped into the car again first, SPORT finally decided to follow her and he went into the car too and Markus could drive home with them.

Since this incident, SPORT would refuse to get near Markus for a long time. Instead he always kept a healthy distance, staying close to either George or myself if Markus was around. He did not want to go anywhere with him anymore. Needless to say that this was the only and the last time that we let SPORT be taken out by anyone else. And it took SPORT several years before he allowed Markus to pet him again.

Stone Fences

During our many walks we often passed by some brick fences, some lower, some higher. SPORT – just like some children do – insisted on walking on top of any of these walls. If he was not able to jump on it himself, he tried and nagged as long until we lifted him up on it. Then he would proudly strut along the top of the wall like a conqueror, watching the world from a higher place. And he fought off any attempt of us to grab and take him back down if we thought the wall had become too uneven and high. We did not want him to fall off and hurt himself. But SPORT could be very hard-headed, he had his own ways and rather jumped off the wall by himself. Which he could do very elegantly, Schnauzers are great jumpers.

During one of our outings, SPORT got on this low stone wall, happily balancing along. As this wall became gradually higher and higher from section to section, SPORT reached the point where we wanted him back down. But SPORT had more adventures on his mind, and instead of jumping off on our side of the wall, he took a quick leap down the other side before we could grab him. The wall was circling a large office complex with a grassy area around the building. That was where he wanted to snoop and romp around on his own while ignoring us calling him.

We watched this stubborn rascal for a while and then decided to teach him a lesson and disappear from his sight. Perhaps this would make him look for us instead, switching positions. And bingo, this worked sure enough! A short time later we saw him searching for us. But from his position the wall was blocking him from coming back on our side again, it was too high. So SPORT ran up and down alongside the wall, becoming kind of nervous when he could not find a way to come back over. At that point, we called his attention and encouraged him to follow us down to the beginning of the wall where it was low enough again for him to spring up on it and thus come over to our side. *"Well, we hope this taught you something, Bighead!"* we greeted him. SPORT looked at us somewhat confused and embarrassed and decided to stay put for the remainder of the outing.

All-Weather-Dog?

SPORT was a cool-weather dog. If it was dry, sunny and cool, then this was his element. He would happily strut around. If it happened to be rainy, he usually kept laying on his favorite place at home, playing deaf or dumb as if he did not understand that it was his time for a walk. Although we normally waited until the rain stopped or wore down a bit before we took SPORT outside, it sometimes could not be avoided walking him during such unpleasant conditions. Then he would stop right outside the door, having this look on his face as if to say *"is this really necessary?",* but he followed us, though reluctantly. Or he decided that he did not want to take up with this and simply turned around after half a block, aiming back home again. But this did not help him much, as on such occasions he was put on the leash. He never tried to fight this, but instead walked well-mannered alongside, however sulking a bit. Arriving at the grassy area in the neighborhood, he could run freely again. But the wet grass and muddy walkway irked him. He resorted to tiptoeing on the curbstone of the sidewalk, sour-faced. *"Good grief, SPORT, you really act like a prissy city dog."* Anyway, we sort of understood his dislike of getting his feet muddy and we had to chuckle about his behavior.

At other times when there happened thunder or even lightening moving in from afar, SPORT was in a real hurry to get back home. He would stop in his tracks, look at me and turn his head in the direction of home, several times over. And he was right, this was no time to be out there too long. So, on such occasions, we did not linger around for long and saw to it to get back home rather soon.

SPORT usually suffered during summer time when the weather turned warm. He did not take hot weather too well. He just dragged along, always seeking a shady area. In the park, he preferred to rest comfortably in the shade of a tree or bush, just contentedly watching what was going on around him.

At one area of the park, there was this small flat pond surrounding a little fountain. SPORT always walked around it on the low stone fence, taking a sip of water if he was thirsty, but he would never jump into it like some other dogs might have loved to do. SPORT was not too fancy about the wet element. But one day, when it was especially hot, George succeeded in luring him into the water. They had been playing with a small stick, which George finally dropped into the pond – unintentionally of course – or not? SPORT, longing to get to the desired stick, stuck one of his front paws into the water, pulling it back quickly, shaking it *"yuk!"* But seeing the stick swaying on top of the water right in front of him, he could not resist any longer. SPORT at last stepped down into the pond, slowly, one leg after the other, trying to get hold on the low bottom. Now he was standing in the water, which barely reached up to his belly. SPORT seemed not to know whether to make a sour face or to enjoy the coolness of the water. It felt so strange. He turned around to look at George. *"It's all right, Sport. This feels great, doesn't it? Now go and get your stick."* Slowly and carefully,

SPORT waded over to the stick and grabbed it with his mouth. Cautiously, he kept moving and stalking around in the water, still skeptical whether it was the right thing to do. It was funny to watch him, knowing that he had no particular liking of getting wet, but then again seeing in his face how unsure he was whether he should admit that the water actually made him feel better in this hot weather and so pleasantly cooled him off. He decided that he liked it. After a while – when he had enough of it - SPORT came out of the pond, shook his fur and walked off with his rescued stick.

Ever since that time, SPORT wanted to pay a visit to this fountain if the weather was hot. He had learned the good side of cool water and he volunteered to step into it. But he would never race splish-splashing around, he always either played the flamingo just standing still on one spot or he simply stalked carefully to and forth in the pond several times.

And then there was also wintertime with all its snow. We could not wait introducing SPORT to his first experience with this frozen powdery substance. How would he react? It had been snowing heavily the night before and there was a thick layer of snow on the ground. We were eager to take SPORT out to this winter wonderland. When he first walked into the snow he stopped, being startled, sniffing at this strange and cool matter. What was this? We encouraged him to come on, formed a snowball and rolled it in front of him. SPORT took a leap to catch it and sunk into the deep snow up to his elbows and knees. *"Oh, what have they got me into this time?"* He was puzzled but seemed to enjoy this. With sparkles in his eyes and a wide smile on his face, he kept jumping into the snow around him, swishing around with his front legs, stirring and swirling it up and chasing and biting the flakes that were falling down. Most of all he loved for us to throw snowballs for him to fetch, not understanding why they melted and disappeared in his mouth while trying to hold on to them. Or he watched in amazement how they busted into a cloud of flakes when he smacked them too hard with his front paws. This all was a new experience for SPORT and he showed his joy in giving us some gleeful barks, snow sticking all over his face, to his long eyebrows and to his beard, while wildly wagging his stumpy tail. SPORT was having a good time!

But winter was not always so pleasant. Depending on the condition of the weather and how sticky the snow was, SPORT sometimes had a problem with the snow becoming clogged and sticking tightly to the hair between the pads on his feet. When this happened, the snow turned into an icy mass which was very difficult to remove outside in the cold and SPORT had a hard time walking on these frozen lumps. It became so bad one time that SPORT began to whine, holding his feet up in my direction, lamenting loudly. So I picked the poor fellow up on my arms and carried him about a block until we reached home. Even other people passing by became sympathetic and asked *"oh, what's wrong with him, is he injured?"*

In order to avoid this bothersome condition, we learned to put Vaseline on his pads before leaving the house. This would also protect him from the salt that was put out there in the neighborhood to make the snow melt on the sidewalks. Salt can be very damaging and painful to a dog's feet, especially if there happen to be minor cracks and injuries on his pads after walking on gravel or other uneven surfaces. That's also why we usually gave SPORT's feet a quick rinse after coming home during wintertime, thus taking care of any salty residue. This and a little Vaseline rubbed onto his pads before going outside took care of the problem and made us have some pleasant and happy ventures in the snow.

Riding the Car

SPORT also loved to ride in the car. If he was alone in there with George, he would sit proudly on the front passenger seat enjoying it, especially if George reached over to pet him. If I happened to ride with them, then I would occupy the front passenger seat and this usually annoyed SPORT, as he considered this his reserved place. In the beginning I took him on my lap, but this seemed not to be too comfortable for him. So he usually moved down to the foot area, complaining. Over time, though, he accepted this set-up, then sit or lay on the back seat, where he moved around from one window to the other, flirting with other drivers or passengers in the lanes next to us. He loved for us to roll the window down a bit so that he could rest his snout on the opening, holding his nose into the wind. His facial hair being blown back by the wind, ears flying, SPORT looked like Snoopy sitting on his dog house pretending to be the WWII Flying Ace, only head cap, waving shawl and big goggles were missing. Being unromantic, however, we did not allow this too often, as we did not want him to catch a cold or get irritated eyes.

Another favored position of SPORT was to stand up on the back seat and reach over to the front seat and lay his head or paws on George's shoulder in front of him. This was heartwarming to watch, as it seemed to be part of their bonding. It was evident how really close SPORT felt to his beloved alpha-man, and George gleefully reached back with one hand to rub SPORT's head. Yes, this was his buddy, his road partner, they were inseparable and belonged to each other!

SPORT knew his surroundings very well, he knew exactly in what area we were just driving and where we would usually take a turn. If we passed by the one exit leading to the big park, however, he would raise hell if the car did not take the desired turn and instead went on going another direction. Very displeased, he kept whining or sometimes even bark at us, trying to make us aware that we were going the wrong direction. *"No, Bighead, this time we are not going to visit the rabbits, we will be going somewhere else today."* He did not particularly like this idea, but eventually settled down again and was soon engaged in watching other interesting actions going on outside the car.

Bus and Subway Stations

Being underway with SPORT called for our full attention. If we happened to pass by a bus stop with a bus waiting, doors wide open, SPORT took this as an invitation to hop on, his master following or not. We realized his special preference after George once had to get him off the bus the last minute before the doors closed up and the bus left. SPORT just loved to ride.

In a subway station there are stairs and escalators. Dogs are not allowed on the escalator, for good reasons, as their paws could get painfully squashed. So SPORT, being a good dog, would run up the stairs while George or I used the escalator. And SPORT, living up to his name, would usually turn this basically boring event into an exciting happening. He raced up as fast as he could, zigzagging between the other passengers who were wondering where his master could be. Of course SPORT reached the top before we did, then standing there wide-legged, watching us slowly moving up, waiting and grinning, his stumpy tail and whole body wiggling of joy "*I am first, I am first!*"

Automatic Glass Door

During the time SPORT was discovering the wonders of the outside world, one particular thing caught his special interest. An office building in the neighborhood had a set of glass doors. We were standing in the entrance in front of the door while I was reading an information sheet at the wall. SPORT was sniffing around and all of a sudden, the glass door opened. Startled, he jumped back. Nobody went in or came out. What was this? And what is it now, the door is closing back up again! SPORT threw me a puzzled look. He moved closer to the door once more, investigating. Now the door opened anew, and closed again when he stepped back. Strange, nobody was around! He seemed to realize that it had something to do with himself. So he kept on walking toward the door, opening it that way and, while retreating, having it close again, repeating it over and over. SPORT began to enjoy this, he had discovered the automatic door! Whenever we happened to walk past this building at a later time, he remembered what he could do and the fun he had with it and wanted to make it happen again. He would nudge me, pointing his head in the intended direction until I would take him over there.

SPORT goes Shopping

We took SPORT along with us as often as we could. He was welcome in most of the shops that we frequented, except perhaps the supermarket. There he had to wait outside. Usually we did not tie his line to the devices outside the store meant to hold any visiting pets, because he stayed put if we told him so. He would be standing there, curiously following us with his eyes into the catacombs of the many supermarket isles and happily greeting us when we reappeared.

This one day, though, George was getting his shopping done when he heard someone ask, *"Whose dog is this?"* George turned around and there he was, SPORT was walking nonchalantly – *"tee tada tada"* – down the aisle, looking at the wonderful world of supermarket life and perhaps also for his Georgy. George quickly took him back to the entrance and told him to stay, which he then did. Well, he had only tried. But he was not bored waiting either, as there were always people smiling and talking to him, telling him how cute he was. However, if anyone tried to rub him, he would avoid this, he did not like for strangers to touch him. Exactly this was the reason why we stopped taking him along to the grocery store and letting him wait at the entrance for us to come back out. After we heard that several dogs had disappeared over time waiting outside the store for their owners, we decided not to have SPORT get into any situation like this. It would have broken our hearts – and definitely his too – if anyone had stolen him.

But then there were all the other shops in the neighborhood where the owners liked to see SPORT and usually had a snack waiting for him inside. Naturally, he understood this very quickly and he used to run straight behind the counter to claim his treat. The owners thought this was cute and they were delighted to let him have his way. And every time we walked past any of these shops, SPORT stopped at their entrance, looking at us and then again at the entrance, *"Are we not going inside?"* No, we did not always go inside. As we lived in the middle of the city and there were plenty shops around whose owners were fond of SPORT, our walks would have looked like stop and go, stop and go. There was the pizzeria, and the bakery, the fish store, the pharmacy, the lotto shop, the cleaners or the gas station, SPORT tried to visit as many of his "watering holes" as often as he could. We had to watch it that this would not interfere with his diet and that he would not get too greedy.

This one day, we had just passed by the pharmacy, when I turned around and didn't see SPORT anywhere. He had still been there a second ago, where could he be? All I saw was the automatic glass door of the pharmacy just sliding back again. That's what it was, he had learned before that these kinds of doors opened by themselves if he stood directly in front of them – just like the one at the office building. So today he had tried this again and took the liberty of walking intently straight through the opening door into the pharmacy all alone. I rushed after him, just barely being able to stop him from standing up on his hind legs and slamming his front paws on the counter, looking longingly at the glass jar containing the dog snacks. *"SPORT, you embarrass me!"* But the employees laughed, *"Come on, he is one of our best customers"* and threw him one of the treats they always kept for their canine visitors. I put SPORT on the leash and walked out, shaking my head about this brazing little fellow. From now on SPORT was being kept on the leash before passing by or going into the pharmacy.

At another occasion, when George walked into a pet store downtown, SPORT again showed his independence where shopping was concerned. Right next to the entrance inside the store there was – very strategically placed – a basket full of roasted pig ears. George had already picked some other items he wanted and was standing at the cashier's desk when he looked around, seeing SPORT sticking head over heels in the basket with the pig ears. *"Goodness, SPORT, can't you wait? Come on out of there!"* SPORT wiggled himself back out of the basket and ran over to George, head high up, proudly holding one of the desired pig ears in his mouth. While George was about to pay his merchandise, he teased SPORT, *"What about yours, can you pay for it?"* SPORT looked to the cashier and to George, from one to the other with big wondering and innocent eyes, *"what are you talking about?"* The cashier had to laugh, *"SPORT, is that what your name is? Well, this pig ear is on the house. No pay. Have fun with it!"* And SPORT happily walked out of the store behind George, carrying his bounty, showing off.

It was time to go to the cleaners and pick up some items. The lady in the shop liked SPORT and as always reached behind the counter to get a few munchies for him. And SPORT, expectantly, took these in his mouth. But this time you could see his face slowly turning sour, he looked at the lady somewhat dismayed, and then – *"phooey!"* – spit the treat back out. Both, the cleaning lady and I were quite perplexed, as SPORT had never before rejected a dog treat. We had seen other dogs savor over these very same kinds of tidbits, but not so SPORT, he had become selective. I felt a bit embarrassed, but the lady saw it differently, *"That's okay, dogs are just like little children, they are very straight forward and unabashed in expressing what they like or don't like."* She was absolutely right.

Then there was this pizzeria down at the corner at the end of our block, where we sometimes picked up a take-home dinner when we were too lazy to cook. There was a sign at the door that dogs were not allowed to come inside, so SPORT always waited outside in front of the door of the restaurant. But this time the guy behind the counter asked, *"Who is that?"* pointing at the door, where SPORT was standing, peeking through the glass door to see what was going on inside. *"Is that your dog? Why don't you let him come in, he looks so cute! Never mind the sign out there."* After I let SPORT inside, he stood very well-behaved right next to me, looking around with big eyes, putting his antenna up to take in all the new and appealing smells. *"What does he like to eat? Can I give him some Salami?"* – *"Oh, I'd rather have you not feeding him, as he will forever take advantage of this and would want to come in here every time he passes by. We also have to watch his diet. And Salami would be too salty anyway."* One of the guy's colleagues butted in, *"just look at him, isn't he a charmer?"* By that time, SPORT understood that the talk was all about him and he looked excitedly from one person to the other, his stumpy tail wiggling. *"Come on, Ma'am, I would like to give him a treat. Maybe he likes cheese?" "Okay, but only a small piece,"* I replied. And when the pizza-man flung him a piece of cheese, SPORT jumped and caught it in mid-air. He was crazy about cheese. SPORT was showing his delight with a smile on his face, blinking his eyes and smacking his lips loudly. The pizza-men laughed, they had never seen a dog eating cheese and they thought this was real funny. But before they could keep on throwing pieces of cheese to SPORT, I was glad that the ordered pizza was ready and we could leave the place. I did not want him to be overfed with snacks. And, as envisioned, SPORT was trying to go into this place from now on every time we were in the neighborhood. Sometimes we would still take him there with us, but most of the times not, then of course being asked, where "that cheese-eating dog" of ours was.

The lotto shop down the street was another place where SPORT loved to go. The couple handling it really took a liking to him. We were in there quite often, also just to chat. During the summer, when the entrance door to their shop stood open, we had to watch SPORT, as he had the tendency to walk in there also all alone, even when we did not intend to do so ourselves at that particular time. This couple did not just spoil him with goodies, they also rubbed and petted him and gave him ample attention in talking to him. SPORT enjoyed this, lying half behind the counter, watching everything going on and being content while George and I were speaking to the shop owners. Until the day, when they moved their business to a different part of town and we could not visit them anymore. For some time, the shop was empty and the door locked. SPORT could not comprehend that all of a sudden his friends were gone, he kept stopping at the door, wondering why he could not get in. After a while, some new owners took over, but they were not friendly at all, and SPORT finally understood that this place was better to be ignored.

But there was still the gas station, where George used to gas up his car and buy his paper every morning. SPORT was a welcome guest there too. This place was a must for SPORT to stop and say hello. If ever George happened to come by without his four-legged friend, he would reproachfully be asked, *"Where is your dog?"* George and SPORT were an acknowledged team in the neighborhood and if one of them was without the other, people became curious and asked.

If I was walking SPORT, I was often stopped by people that I had seen before only on a distance, but did not really meet yet. They wanted to know whether this was SPORT, whom they had seen only to be together with George. There were two or three other Standard Schnauzers living in the extended neighborhood though, but all of them had a black coat and were not pepper-and-salt like SPORT, except perhaps for Gipsy. So, George and SPORT were well known all around.

Training

When George took SPORT outside and gave him his training sessions, Gipsy went with them many times. As she was already thoroughly trained and knew by herself what to do and when, this was of great benefit to SPORT. He did not only listen to the directions of George, but also saw how Gipsy acted, and he learned a lot from her. It was absolutely essential that he learned to obey on the first call as he was living in a city environment with traffic and a lot of other distractions. We thought, praising him when he did something right was more effective than scolding him if he did something wrong, although this was of course also necessary occasionally, mostly in order to stop him from getting hurt. But this little fellow was smart, he made us proud, as he really began to understand the rules and had himself under control and listened to us when we called.

SPORT enjoyed being shown different situations and chores and was eager to do them right. It really seemed to be the highlight of his day when he was praised for having done a job well.

Although we walked him on the leash many times, especially in crucial situations, we believed in letting him go without it more often. If we decided to put him on the line though, he did not particularly like it, but he never pulled or dragged behind. Instead he walked well-mannered alongside us. However, sometimes he showed his disdain in reaching over to the leash, grabbing it in his mouth as if to take the leadership away from us, giving us this look *"Hey, I can walk alone, I don't need this. You should know better than that."*

The very first time I took him out alone, I was not so sure how he would respond to me, as I was not the one who had trained him. But George assured me that it was okay. He fully trusted his dog, and he was not wrong. When SPORT and I were walking alone, he usually behaved quite orderly. He completely accepted my lead, actually expecting my command. Waiting at the curb of the street for the cars to pass, he stood there, impatiently though, looking up at me, anticipating the magic word – my command. If – in his mind – it took too long, he would give me a few barks. He seemed like a running motor, ready to shoot ahead. But he would not go before I told him so or I would do the first step myself.

Walking SPORT in the city and walking him without a leash made it necessary to be extra careful and be aware and alert in any situation. This way, SPORT also had me trained indirectly the other way around. While I used to cross the streets more or less careless before, I was very cautious now, as there was the added responsibility of looking out for my dog. I kept this behavior also when SPORT happened not to be with me. SPORT would have been proud of himself for having influenced me in such a way.

I had been walking SPORT on this stretch of greenery with several streets crossing it. He was running in front of me, and – very well behaved – stopping at every crossing. Standing there, waiting for me to catch up, he occasionally looked back to see where I was. People sometimes stopped and watched, perhaps afraid that he might run into the street, which he never did. *"Well, he really is trained well,"* they used to praise him. But not everything came as easy as it might have looked. SPORT was quite headstrong and often there was a struggle on who would succeed in having his way.

Raining on his Parade

For a while – when SPORT was still quite young – I used one of those thin leashes that you could extend or pull back into a flat box-like handgrip, whatever was needed in a situation. This was a big mistake. SPORT demonstrated clearly what he thought of such a device. A friend of mine and her dog Monty – a pretty Westhighland Terrier – and SPORT and I were walking in the park this one day. There was a carnival going on nearby with a lot of people and commotion, so we had to keep our dogs on the leash for them not to get lost or being trampled on. But SPORT, getting this pleasing scent of food in his nose, very curiously wanted to be right in the middle of it all, doing his own excursions. He grabbed the leash in his mouth, looked at me from the side, very well knowing that he was about to do something bad and went on chew, chew, chew. And before I could get a hold of him, the line was through and SPORT gone. However, his taste buds and his greed for some goodies made it possible for me to catch him again real quickly. There was this group of guys eating something, and standing right with them I spied SPORT, putting on his best beg. They were talking and joking with him and SPORT was so consumed by their attention that he did not notice me sneaking up on him. I could grab him at his collar, putting the torn leash back on with a knot. He did not like this too much and tried again to bite the leash off, but big sister was watching him. *"Sorry that I have to rain on your parade, buddy, but if you behave like this we will go a different route."* After this outing, I got him another type of leash, one out of strong leather that he could not chew through so easily. He outgrew the chewing-age, but he developed other ways of letting me know when he had something different on his mind.

Bighead

If he did not want to go a certain way, he simply stopped, just standing there, making no move to go on. *"Come on, SPORT"*, I would call to him. But he was persistent, he pointed his head into the direction he wanted to go instead, then looked at me full of hope and again to his intended direction, repeating this a few times. If I gave in, he would happily shoot away to where he thought he had to check some traps, to see if perhaps a stranger had invaded his territory, or to pick up the news from some fellow canines or he left a message himself. If I proceeded my own way, he grudgingly followed me, but many times he would just sit or lay down, indicating his un-

willingness to come on. People passing had to grin over this hard headed fellow, watching how this dispute would be settled. I usually just kept on walking, and SPORT would follow after a while when the distance seemed to get too far.

But sometimes he insisted on having his will, just sitting there and keeping an eye on me from a distance. I did not have a loud voice and was not about to shout all across half of the city for him to come. And – to my dismay – I could not whistle either. For that reason I developed some kind of sign language for SPORT to follow. When he acted up like this, I would fling my hand, pointing with my finger to the ground next to me. Somehow he quickly understood that this was his last chance before being scolded. So he usually obeyed immediately, then of course being greeted with a *"good boy, SPORT, good boy."* And we were friends again.

Aside from these little power games, SPORT was the most lovable guy you could think of. He may have seemed rugged on the outside, but inside of him there was a very tender and sensitive soul. And this tender soul needed to be nourished. SPORT was very affectionate, but only with George or me and perhaps a few close friends. He loved for us to pet him, talk and smooch and rub cheeks with him. But if a stranger wanted to stroke him, SPORT would most of the time move just out of reach, he did not like for strangers to get too close. He was not afraid or unfriendly then, perhaps distant and careful. Sometimes on our walks, small children stopped and asked if I would allow them to pet SPORT. *"Well, let's ask him first if he wants to be rubbed today",* I generally told them, explaining that not all dogs like this, especially if they don't know the person. Although SPORT was not always exactly fond of this procedure, he usually held still after I bent down to him, convincing him with some reassuring words that it was okay. And while I stood by, rubbing the side of his neck, watching that he would not change his mind, he let the wondering and happily smiling child pat him carefully and get a sense of what a dog feels like. However, SPORT, who really had no particular dislike for children and at other times actually loved to sniff and get the scent of little babies in their carriages, still gave me those looks from the side *"do you think that I am a guinea pig?"* And when he had enough he simply walked off. It was like it often happens with small children. If they are supposed to give their hand to greet a stranger or take a hug or a kiss from a little-liked relative, they refuse.

Order of Ranks

SPORT's relationship to George was different to the one he had with me. George was his absolute hero, his alpha person, and his numero uno. He never questioned George's command. That what George said, was the law. I was more like a buddy to SPORT, who sometimes respected me and at other times challenged me for the rank behind George. This showed especially, when George and I walked SPORT together. When we were getting ready to cross a street after the cars had passed and George said *"okay, let's go"*, SPORT would do something that he never tried when he was walking alone with me. He dashed ahead, then sometimes stopped, coming back, barking at me and chasing me while snapping at my legs, *"go on, go on, George said let's go."* Or he would grab my pant legs and try to drag me across the street. In one way, it was really funny how he tried to enforce the command of the alpha-man. On the other hand, fully understanding what he was trying to do, I had to make it clear to him what the order of ranks was in our pack and that I was not going for this behavior. It took quite a number of bruises on my legs and several more shouting matches with him, before he gave this up.

Also, there were those other situations, when SPORT thought, he was the boss. We were just ready to go for a walk, outside the apartment door, when he got into the habit of grabbing my wrist in his mouth, very carefully though, but nevertheless putting a real strong grip on it, trying to lead me to the stairs. And, while slowly tightening his clamp more and more, he glanced at me from the side and his very intense look seemed to be saying, *"I am the one who is going to walk you, sister, and not the other way around. And anyway, hurry up!"* Oh boy, this dog was beginning to suffer from illusion of grandeur. Although chuckling inside about this brazing little fellow, I firmly made him understand that this was not the way to deal with me, that he either had to cut this out or he was to stay at home! And, you guessed it, he eventually stopped playing the macho, and chalked it up as just having tried.

Body Guard

However, having a strong-willed dog sometimes proved to be also reassuring. SPORT was extremely protective of me, and I did not fear walking him in the evenings, even in darker areas. He was an easygoing and good-natured fellow, but he would have immediately attacked anyone trying to harm me. Although SPORT was only of medium height, he was still big enough to interfere in any wrongdoing and scare away any potential aggressor.

This one day he proved his guarding behavior in a rather harmless situation. While I was walking toward a mailbox to put a letter in, a man was coming from the opposite side to do the same. SPORT obviously took this as an act of aggression toward me, ran over to this person, stopped in front of him and gave him a warning growl. I called SPORT back immediately. He behaved grudgingly, coming back to me, still chewing on his growl. The man took it lightly, though, saying *"I understand your dog, if I were him, I would protect you too"* and walked away, smiling.

Another situation was rather funny to me, but I suppose only to me. I had gone into this fish store in the neighborhood and SPORT was waiting outside. When I was finished and ready to walk out of the shop, I came upon this hilarious situation. SPORT was blocking the door, not letting anyone else into the store and keeping a mailman at bay who was hiding behind his cart. Two or three other persons were standing outside discussing what to do. SPORT did not growl or show any aggression. He was just standing there, giving people the look *"hey, you can't come in here right now, it's my owner's turn first."* The people did not know him and therefore were not sure what he might do if they tried to pass him. *"Bighead, I honor your intentions, but this is going too far. Come on, let's go."* I apologized to the mailman and the waiting people and left the location quickly, however secretly chuckling about the scene.

But one evening, the situation we happened to be in was nothing to chuckle about. We were already on our way back home, when suddenly a large black longhaired dog sprinted from somewhere out of the dark toward us, full speed. Good grief, where was the owner, what were we going to do, he looked so vicious! It all happened so fast! When the big dog reached us, snarling aggressively, SPORT exploded into a fire-spitting dragon. He lunged at him, trying to defend us, biting at the other's throat and flanks. They were furiously dancing around each other, attempting to grab the other at a weak spot.

The big dog had a thick long and shaggy coat, which was not easily to be penetrated by the bites of a much smaller SPORT, who had the disadvantage of just having been trimmed the other week and now being somewhat bare of a protecting pelt. I really feared for him to get injured. But SPORT was fast, very fast! The big aggressor could not get hold of him. They were not listening to my shouts to stop and there was no chance of tearing them apart, as this whirling and snarling ball of fighting canines was always moving just out of reach.

Meanwhile the owner of the other dog had arrived at the scene and she was just as helpless as I was. From two sides, we quietly moved closer to the brawling dogs, trying to soothe them down, and when they finally halted for a moment to catch some breath, we had our chance to grab each dog by the collar, holding them firmly and dragging them apart. To our relief, neither of the dogs was injured, surprisingly, as this fight was absolutely vicious.

As far as the dogs were concerned, it was not over yet, they still tried to get at each other and we had a hard time quieting them down while walking away in different directions. Never before had I seen SPORT being so fearless and fighting so relentlessly! He did not care whether the other dog was so much bigger than he was himself; he just wanted to protect his pack. While I was walking us home, still having week knees, I was awfully proud of my brave dog!

Then there came this evening when SPORT and I were doing our routine walk along a neighborhood alley. During daytime, this alley looked harmless and inviting, people walking with or without their dogs, villas with front yards and big chestnut trees lining both sides of the walkway, which led to a tiny castle surrounded by a small lake, populated by a myriad of ducks. But in the evenings, this place was rather empty, dark and lonely. As SPORT and I had been walking here many times before and had never encountered anything out of the norm, perhaps occasionally running into another dog owner, we also thought nothing about it this particular evening.

It was a bit later than we usually took our walk and there was not a soul underway. We were at about the last third of the stretch when SPORT started to act differently. His hair began to stand up straight from his neck all along his back toward his tail, and he gave off this real dangerously sounding, still somewhat suppressed, yet warning growl. He began to stalk cautiously, apparently ready to charge. I was on red alert! Even though I did not see anyone, I trusted SPORT's instincts. When he behaved like this, there must be something wrong.

The situation was eerie, totally quiet and nobody around. But something was up! This was hair-raising, I put a harder grip on a stick that I had picked up earlier and was still carrying, just in case I needed something for defense. Perhaps someone was hiding behind one of those large trees?

And then, sure enough, when we approached this particular chestnut tree, there a guy stepped out from behind it, doing what all flashers do, open his coat and expose his family jewels. SPORT moved closer to this tree, blocking the guy off, now growling loudly and openly at this creep. SPORT was standing there, quivering with hostility, just waiting for the guy to make another move, a sign to charge.

I let the guy see that I had this stick so that he could envision a possible whopping if he dared anything else. But I kept on walking my normal pace, trying to make it look as if I was ignoring him. I did not want to give this guy the satisfaction of having scared me. But from the corner of my eyes I nevertheless peeked to see whether he would step out of his hideout any further and come toward us. However, it seemed that SPORT's highly aggressive posture had ruined this guy's day. He did not move from his spot, surely out of fear to ignite SPORT's attack.

By now I was past the tree and the flasher – the end of the alley was now close – so I called SPORT to come on. It looked as if he had put enough fear in this guy for him to avoid this area in the future, as we never saw him again. SPORT ran over to me, still grumbling and highly agitated. I praised him for so bravely protecting me and keeping the guy at bay, but it took him quite a while before he calmed down again. There was still an occasional growl coming from his throat while we were walking home. But eventually he put the incident behind him, his hair stopped standing up and he was his normal self again.

There was yet another – indirect – way that SPORT looked out for me. This was usually on his excursions together with George. As both of them were well known and liked in the neighborhood, they were stopped many times to have a chat. If it happened to be a woman who talked to them, SPORT would watch this for a while, then eventually butt in when the talk seemed to take too much time. He would nudge George, grab his pant legs and try to pull him away, or he would give a *woof* or two, indicating that it was enough and George should walk on. George used to tease me about this frequently, letting me know that SPORT had protected my interests again. SPORT did not tolerate any other women near my man if I was not around. Yes, I could really depend on my dog!

Rebellious Times

Just as youths of the human species, dogs definitely go through a phase too where they seem to forget their entire good behavior. SPORT truly was a lovable little rascal, but if he got a wild hair in his butt, he could really make you wonder. He was taught, not to pick up anything eatable off the street or to drink out of a puddle, or take anything from a stranger. He was also taught to follow immediately when called by us. And he used to abide by the set rules. But there came these times where he simply had to provoke us.

The Puddle

It had been raining the night before. We were walking in the park and came upon a large puddle. Although knowing that he was not allowed to take a slurp out of it, he ran up to the glittering water, and while bending down as if to drink he gave us this look from the side. *"No, SPORT, no. We warn you!"* And there it was, this sparkle in his eyes. We just knew that he was up to something. He galloped around the puddle to the other side, stopped and looked over to us, making sure that we saw what he was doing. He knew we could not get to him fast enough to stop him. So he did a few slurps and grinned at us from across, *"I got you this time, ha?"* And as soon as we made a move toward him, he took off, ran a few yards, lingered, turned around to see that a certain distance was being kept. He knew very well that he had done something he would be scolded for. But he seemed to enjoy the risk.

Yew Bushes

On our further route through the park, we passed by some yew-bushes. SPORT, curious as he was, had to investigate those little red berries that were sticking to them or had fallen to the ground. Although he had been warned before on earlier outings to stay away from them, these bushes seemed to have a strong fascination to him and he always managed to rush over there before we could get a hold of him and – just because of it – gobble down a few of the berries. Unfailingly, they used to make him sick a little later during the day. He would become nauseated and get the collywobbles, with all the side effects. It took him several belly aches and a lot of scolding to understand that there was a connection between eating those berries and him feeling so bad, and he finally left them alone.

Is he a Rowdy?

Most of the times, SPORT was easygoing and pleasant when being walked, sniffed here and there and was really content. But sometimes, he had a little devil in him. Did someone come along with another dog, big or small, on the leash, I had the impression that SPORT was suddenly growing little horns on his forehead. With a quick glance from the side toward me and a sparkle in his eyes that couldn't mean anything good, he sprinted at high speed toward the other dog – just to push on his breaks and stop barely out of reach of him. Usually, the other owner and his dog were catching their breath in shock, staring at SPORT, thinking that he really wanted to attack them. But this was not at all on SPORT's mind, he simply loved to bluff other dogs this way. More than once, I had to apologize to the other owners, trying to explain that my dog was not about to do any harm. Oh, what an "excuse"! Surely, this phrase has been used too often by dog owners while their dogs were still out to get into a fight with the other one. I knew my dog better, but strangers could not know that.

Once again, I learned a lesson in dealing with my dog. As he was doing this only when he happened to be running free and the other dog was on the leash, I had to catch an upcoming situation like this before SPORT did and put him quickly on his leash. Then everything would be all right, SPORT did not even pull at his line. If the other dog ran free, though, and SPORT was on the leash, I used to release him too, and they simply sniffed at each other to greet. That way, neither of the dogs felt superior over the other. At least this is what I believe was the reason behind such behavior, as I had seen other dogs do the same.

The Sandbox

SPORT was not always the initiator of naughty behavior, though. George and I could be called guilty of this ourselves. We knew that SPORT went absolutely crazy when he had a sandy ground under his feet. So sometimes in the evenings, when there was nobody around to see us, we let SPORT go wild in the sandbox of a playground. Shame on us, but it was just too great to watch SPORT releasing his feelings of joy. He went in there, zigzagging to and forth, *"yap, yap, yap"*. He kept on running, digging, racing all across; he just could not get enough of this strange and ticklish feeling of sand under his feet. He simply loved it and when he finally came out, he rewarded us with the happiest expression on his face, his stumpy tail wagging like mad.

The Trickster

Sometimes he tried to trick us, playing the innocent. We had just been on a pleasant outing and were on our way back home. As he normally ran well in front of us, we could always keep a good look over him. Now and then, though, he seemed to be dragging behind without any apparent reason. This was the time to be suspicious. Just like on this sunny Sunday afternoon, SPORT had slowed down and lingered somewhere behind us *"SPORT, come here",* we called him. *"What's going on, buddy?"* He looked at us, not quite holding his head up as he normally did. But the extra and overdrawn expression of innocence on his face told us that he was trying to hide something. This little trickster knew that we would not approve of whatever he was hiding. He was sending some quick and harmless glances up into the sky and to some remote area as if to put our attention on something else. But we had already noticed it. Why did his beard stick out at the sides of his face more than normally and did not fall straight down as usual? It seemed to cover something underneath. *"Hey, SPORT, you think you are slick, ha? Do you really believe you could get away with this? Pfui!!".* The key word "*pfui!*" made him obey immediately and spit out whatever he was holding in his mouth. He gave us this heart-tearing look, he would have loved so much to eat this piece of chicken bones he had just found. "*No way, SPORT, the risk is too great that it might be spiked.*" The city paper too often reported about incidents where dog-hating creeps tried to harm our four-legged buddies. We did not want to take any chances. SPORT did one more try, turned around and jumped on this piece of chicken to pick it up again. A firm *"No, SPORT, no!"* stopped him and he walked on, head down. We rubbed his back, promising him that he would have some other goodies after getting back home.

Learning it the hard way

There were some lessons that SPORT had to learn the hard way. One of those happened on one of his favorite walking routes. In our neighborhood, there was this overpass across a street with quite some heavy traffic. We used to walk over it from a green strip on one side to a small park-like landscape on the other side. Normally, SPORT enjoyed to look down onto the passing traffic from far above on this overpass. But this particular day, he must have had another wild hair somewhere. Instead of following right behind George walking up the stairs to the overpass, he must have figured that he wanted to surprise George and meet him half way from the other side of the bridge. For that he had to cross the busy street below.

When George realized that there were none of SPORT's familiar scraping footsteps behind him, it was already too late. There was this agonizing sudden void, where was SPORT? George's heart almost stopped when he heard a whimpering coming from the other side of the street. There, SPORT was lying at the curbstone, cars speeding past him. George raced over to him, not bothering about the traffic himself, fearing the worst. He grabbed SPORT, trying to help him up, examining him for injuries. SPORT was shaking like a leaf, but he was able to stand on all four feet. There was real fear in his eyes. He was in shock.

George tried to soothe him while he was still checking for any possible lacerations or sensitive spots. There were none, it was a miracle. It seemed as if SPORT had been lucky and got away uninjured. But the horror of zigzagging between these racing vehicles and avoiding collision with them had put a real scare into him. SPORT would never again try to cross a busy street alone. The terror of this incident was engraved in his head forever.

Grooming

SPORT did surprise me. As someone who was used to having cats around and knowing how clean they are, constantly grooming and taking care of their furs, I was truly astounded to see SPORT doing this in a similar manner. I had never thought about dogs cleaning themselves that way, this was a cat's thing. But of course, all animals are naturally clean. When left in their natural habitat, they will by instinct do everything to stay healthy and that includes cleanliness. If it means rolling in the dust or mud to be protected from the sun or keep insects off their body, then that is part of their grooming. That might not exactly be a human's fancy, but it still serves its purpose for some creatures. Surely, to go this far was not necessary for SPORT – or almost not, but this is a different story to be told later.

When SPORT came in from a walk outside or after a messy dinner, he liked to settle down in his nest or on his bunk in the back room and then start to lick and clean his fur and paws. He did not leave out an area as far as he could reach. Just like a cat, he used to wet his paw and rub it over his face and ears, causing the hair to get tousled but clean. When doing this, he looked real cute, laying there, feeling content and happy, having a smile on his face. Yes, our dog could actually smile!

As far as SPORT was concerned, this was well enough for the sake of grooming. But being a Schnauzer, he was supposed to be stripped and trimmed three to four times a year. While he was still a puppy, we tried as long as possible to brush and comb him to keep his wiry hair untangled and manageable, also to prepare him for what he had to face later on. And after a few months, the day had come where his first stripping and trimming was due.

It was a mess. Markus had suggested a guy who was doing this professionally. It was supposed to take place at our home, in SPORT's familiar environment. We had set up a table, on top of which SPORT was to be placed during the procedure. Now, stripping and trimming – meaning the plucking of any loose hair and at the same time cutting all of the tight hair with a special tool – is not exactly a pleasant procedure to some dogs. Others actually like it, though, as it relieves them of some surplus hair, which in previous times would have been ripped out naturally during hunting in the underbrush. If his hair would not be removed, the old or dead hair roots could draw bacteria and cause illnesses to the dog over time – at least this was explained to us by the trimmer.

Little innocent SPORT had no idea what was coming. Even though the guy tried to make friends with him before he started, SPORT immediately began to growl at him when he put his hands on him to shear and clip his hair. We had to interfere and quiet the little fellow down, trying to make it look as a normal and regular process that wasn't anything to get upset about. But SPORT was so adversely excited that he peed on himself. He just hated it that a stranger was fumbling all over his body. And the humming electric shears did not exactly calm him down either. To top it off, SPORT was slightly nicked during the process. This really gave it all a bad start. We had to hold and comfort poor little SPORT during the whole treatment. He was really intimidated. After the guy left, we tried to build up SPORT's ego again. We just hoped that SPORT would eventually get used to this procedure, understanding that this would not harm him in any way and actually could make him feel better after getting rid of his thick fur, especially during summer time.

Scaled Herring

After this first trimming was finished, I thought, '*my goodness, this guy made him look like a scaled herring.*' SPORT looked so naked, I had the urge to put my arms around him to keep him warm. All the puppy-like fuzziness was gone. But then again, his appearance had become more mature. His beard had been growing during recent times and the guy had accentuated it very nicely, it was very attractively standing out against the rest of the trimmed fur.

Also, now while the hair had been shortened, we could notice that his body was developing into the rather square and solid Schnauzer figure with his muscles beginning to show under the neatly trimmed pelt. The hair was left a bit longer on his

front legs toward the paws, giving him a strong and sturdy look. After two or three weeks, SPORT's hair had grown a bit again and the naked look disappeared. By now we all had become used to his changed appearance and we had to admit, SPORT was growing into a real handsome fellow!

Second Try

A month or so later, when George and his buddy happened to walk into Markus' barbershop, SPORT became really upset, his hair raised and he began to growl at a person sitting in there. It was the guy who had done his trimming earlier. SPORT was still misgiving and he did not want this man to come near him again. It was clear to us that we had to look for another person to do SPORT's hair. And we found one before the next grooming was due. It was a young woman – Petra was her name –who had specialized in trimming Terriers and Schnauzers. She had a little shop not too far away where she was grooming her four-legged customers professionally. So next time SPORT needed a haircut, George and I went there together with him to see how he was dealing with it.

Petra first took her time to make SPORT familiar with herself and the strange surroundings. She played and sweet-talked with him, and SPORT seemed to accept her. But when he finally stood on top of the table, he became somewhat uneasy. We rubbed and assured him that it was okay, that we were watching over him and that we would not let anything bad happen to him. And reluctantly he held still, clinging to us with big wide eyes while allowing Petra to do her work. After she was finished, she awarded him with a well-deserved goody and the world was in order again for him. He forgot all his previous agony and strutted proudly around on our way home, flashing his newly trimmed appearance.

Petra took pride in her work and she really did a good job on SPORT. She knew how to cut his hair in order to accentuate all the positive sides of his looks. As the pepper and salt color of Schnauzers results from a combination of black and white hairs as well as single hairs being banded black and white, the outcome of a haircut was sometimes darker and sometimes lighter, depending on how short the hair was cut. That way, Petra could also make the shades vary at certain areas of SPORT's body. Neck and chest appeared lighter and on the sides of his shoulders there was a slightly lighter shaded band going down along his rib cage to right behind his front legs while the shoulders and back were kept darker in tone. The hair on the legs was sculptured perfectly. On the front and upper part of the elbow it was clipped fairly short while it increased somewhat in length on the back and further down toward the paws, same thing on his hind legs. The hair on SPORT's chest was also kept a bit longer, running slightly bushy from his lower chest toward his belly and decreased again in length in an even line toward the flank area, this way intensifying the intended sturdy Schnauzer-look. His long eyebrows were evened out and fell just barely over his eyes, slightly pointed in the middle and sloped at the sides so that his eyes had room to see better. And when SPORT looked at you from under these eyebrows with his brownish almond-shaped eyes, flashing his beautiful whiskers and beard, and having his neatly trimmed facial hair appearing like a dark mask, you had to admit that he was in good hands, as Petra knew how to groom our dog well.

Zombie

Anyway, since SPORT had still been a bit agitated during the trimming procedure, Petra suggested giving him a mild tranquilizer next time. We talked to the vet about this and he had no objections and actually thought this would make it easier for SPORT. So he handed us a few Valiums and told us to give SPORT a quarter of a pill about an hour before having his hair done. When the time had come, we did as the vet had told us, but we were skeptical. SPORT became tired very soon and he seemed to be in a daze. Then Petra called and postponed the appointment until an hour later the same morning. We were worried that the pill would not work through the whole trimming procedure, but she assured us that the effects would last long enough.

She was right, SPORT did not come out of his trance until late that evening, walking around wobbly and unsteady, bumping into everything in his way. He had to sleep the rest of the effects off during the night. We vowed not to do this again to him! Although he hardly recognized it when his trimming took place, this did not justify his condition after taking the pill. No, never again!

Dire Straits

But during his next visit to Petra, SPORT let out the devil in him. This time George had not come along with us, I had gone with him alone. Petra knew that I was a softy where SPORT was concerned and that he might act up in front of me, playing the poor maltreated victim, which he would not have done with George – his alpha-person – being present. So she thought it might be better if she would be alone with him during the grooming session. She had enough experience with dogs, and as SPORT seemed to be at ease with her I did not worry about him, and did not mind taking a walk in the meantime. However, Petra asked me to come and check after a short while, just in case. And then, when I passed by after about five minutes or so, looking through the show window, Petra was in dire straits. She anxiously waived at me to come in.

SPORT was not on top of the table anymore, he was evasively sitting somewhere under a bench in the back, avoiding being caught and being put back on the table again. *"Good grief, Sport,"* I called him, *"she is not going to slaughter you."* Reluctantly, SPORT came to me, throwing some accusing looks at Petra. I had no intention to let him feel sorry for himself, he had to accept that this procedure was going to be a fact of his life and that it was not at all going to hurt him. I lifted him back up on the grooming table, talking to him in a serious voice, but praising him when he stayed put. Grudgingly, he let Petra do her job, all the while not letting me out of his eyesight. And when he was finished, this rascal forgot all about his act, he was all friends again with Petra, he played and made fun with her, let her pet him, and – what else would you expect – claiming the usual treat for his taste buds.

SPORT became a regular customer of Petra during the following years. Although he came willingly to her shop and seemed to have finally accepted these sessions of stripping and trimming, he sometimes became naughty, did not remotely think about holding still and even tried to nip her occasionally, which resulted in Petra resolutely putting a muzzle on him. At one time, Petra – usually being quite patient – became fed up with SPORT's fidgety behavior and she shouted at him. SPORT was absolutely startled and it intimidated him for a long time, and Petra was sorry that this had affected him so deeply, as she actually liked this little rascal.

There was another situation, where she felt that she had to demonstrate and show me that she was not hurting him. SPORT had a thing about his paws. For a while, as soon as she began working on his feet, SPORT started wailing like a little child, and his eyes desperately transmitted *"she is going to butcher me, she is going to butcher me...!"* Petra lifted one of his legs, no tool in her hands, *"look..."* and brushed once across his pads with her bare finger, demonstrating that she was in no way doing anything painful to him. This immediately initiated a storm of lamentations by SPORT, the expression on his face was one of pure torture and he was howling as if being hung by the nails. *"Sport, you are candidate for an academy award, flashing all those acting talents. Now, cut it out, you clown, you will not fool us with this show of dramatic performance!"* SPORT gave me this look, *"what's wrong with you, party pooper, I put on my best act and you don't play along!"* He just resented having someone mess with his feet. He tried a few more times during his later sessions to behave prissy, but gave this up after a while as it did not bring about any changes.

No matter how big a show he put on during these sessions, immediately following them SPORT was buddy-buddy again with Petra. He was not misgiving for any inconveniences before and happily engaged in some play with her and – naturally – receiving his usual reward, a dog biscuit. Sorry to say, that Petra gave up her profession a few years later and closed her shop. Again we had to find another person to have SPORT get adjusted to. But this worked out fine. The new person was also a younger woman, being a big animal-lover, having two cats and three dogs of her own. SPORT liked to go over to her house, snoop around a little while and then get his trimming done. She also did her job well and SPORT always looked good and well taken care of.

Different kind of Grooming

Proud as George and I were about SPORT's appearance, he sometimes had his own opinion on what the word "grooming" meant. When we were out in the park, he occasionally showed this sudden change in his facial expression. The familiar sparkle appeared in his eyes and - slowing down in his trot - he sent this mischievous look to us from the side and then a short glance to some remote place on the grass. Before we realized what was on his mind, SPORT took off and sprinted to this remote spot he had just eyed and threw himself head-over on it, rolling on his back to and fro, to and fro, legs up paddling in the air. He had found a spot smelling irresistibly to him and he simply had to bathe in this pungent odor, covering his body all over with the desired "perfume". That, what SPORT believed smelled so good, was usually a dead bird or frog or something else decomposing. *"Yuk, SPORT, you stink!"*

Needless to say that we tried to stop him from "grooming" himself like this. But whenever we approached him in such a situation, he just ran off a few yards, waited until we were a bit away from the "site of crime" and then raced back to the rotten spot and rolled in it again. He knew that we did not like this and therefore it was a no-no. But his urge to get smelly was stronger. It was no use, SPORT did everything to trick us in this respect and kept on doing his shoulder-throws whenever and wherever he had a chance to. All dogs love to get pungent now and then and it is just a way of their life. So we decided to let him have his fun, but when we came back home, his first walk would lead him into the bathroom, where we put him in the tub for a good soaping-up. And naturally, this was not too much to his liking, but it was the price he had to pay.

The shoulder-throws alone were not the only reason SPORT had the pleasure entitling him to a shower. If it happened to be rainy outside, SPORT naturally came home being so muddy that we had to carry him across the hall into the bathroom in order to spare the rugs in the entrance from becoming soiled by his dirty footprints. SPORT would be standing in the bathtub resigned to the unavoidable while we ran the lukewarm water over his belly, feet and sides and carefully washed his face and beard. If he had been rolling in something smelly, the dog shampoo came into action and the whole of SPORT was soaped up. After such a session, we quickly laid a towel over him to stop him from shaking and splashing the water all over the place, and then lifted him out of the bathtub and placed him on another towel, where we would dry him off.

As little as he liked any water being put on him, as much did he love being rubbed dry. He was actively helping in the process, firming up and pushing his body against the hand rubbing him with the towel. He even voluntarily lifted one leg after the other to make it easier for us to reach the curves. Just before finishing, he started to blink his eyes, indicating that he was feeling good, looking so fresh and squeaky clean. And then he could not stop his running motor any longer, he was ready to shoot off into the living room, wildly blitzing onto the couch, back on the floor, away into the bedroom, hardly missed bumping into George who came to check what all the commotion was about. These were the moments, when we were glad that SPORT was not a Giant Schnauzer and only of the standard size. After these drying-off sessions, SPORT was wound up like a clock. The blitzing around was his way of releasing and expressing his joy, he was simply feeling great.

After a while when he tuned down his temperament and rested, I could finally comb and brush his beard, which he did not like too much because it would twitch him, but needed to be done while it was still damp in order not to tangle up, same for the hair on his feet. As SPORT was – as always – particular prissy about his feet, I tried making a game out of it, turning on some old charm, sweet-talking to him, this way distracting him from the unpleasant but necessary procedure. While his witty eyes were following every move I made they seemed to convey, *"Don't think I let you get away with this, you'll have to pay me dearly! That will cost you at least a roasted pig ear!"* I am sure that he held still only because he knew that following all of this he would be rewarded with some kind of a dog goody. Then he was satisfied and contentedly settled down, perhaps crowned by a round of smooching.

Is SPORT a Star?

Was SPORT a star? Well, in our own eyes he naturally was a star for sure. But what about others? What did they think? Like this guy who was following us around in the park from a distance. He had all this camera equipment hanging over his shoulders and he was shooting one picture after the other of our puppy dog. He seemed to have found his star. We didn't mind as we had only eyes for cute little fluffy SPORT, who was springing around having fun exploring the big wide world. But we would not have been surprised had we seen a picture of SPORT in some magazine one day.

Exactly that happened later after SPORT had matured and had grown into an eye-catching mature Schnauzer. George found a note on his car one day where a photographer from the neighborhood asked him, if she could make some pictures of him and SPORT, as she intended to publish an article in a city journal about dogs and their owners. So it came about, that my two men appeared in the next issue of this magazine on two full-sized pages with pictures and a short background story beside the stories of a few more dog owners. We were surprised of the echo of this article, as a lot of people had read it and approached George how it had come to this. They wanted to know every little detail. Sometime later, the photographer contacted George again for some more pictures, but this time George refused, he was not up to it anymore.

It was amazing how much attention SPORT was drawing when we walked him. Because of the long eyebrows falling in his face and his full whiskers, SPORT looked sort of grim and stern, while in reality this robust fellow was full of fun, mischief and humorous antics. Strangers would stop us, telling us that they had been watching us

in the neighborhood and complimented us on the looks of our dog and how self-assured and well-behaved he was. But was he material for a dog show, as this one lady tried to make us believe? She had been raising Schnauzers herself before and had an eye for a good breed.

While the lady was telling all of this, I was watching SPORT standing there. I was thinking of how much he resented to be shampooed and combed, and having his nails cut and being fuzzed all over like that.

No, he was a real boy, I did not want our dog to go through all of this just for a few minutes of fame. I wanted him to live his life as a real dog, run and chase, roll in something and get raunchy every now and then, get mischievous and do all those things that dogs love to do, but are not necessarily being rewarded by a judge on a dog show. And anyway, when SPORT grinned at you, you could see that one of his teeth had grown out of the row of the otherwise perfect line of teeth. This alone would have downgraded him in the eyes of the judges. Where George and I were concerned, we did not mind, as to us it was like a trademark of SPORT. No, SPORT did not have to worry about being put in a showcase just to lift the ego of his owners.

Inter-Canine Relationships

Gipsy

Yes, and there still was Gipsy. She was the first fellow dog that SPORT had met in his new home environment. Since he had moved in, her outings with George had become less often, and she seemed to have become a bit jealous. When she was visiting in our house, she sometimes tried to take away the toys of a totally annoyed and protesting SPORT. She mildly growled at him, if he dared to want them back. And then – good grief – SPORT did the ultimate fauxpas. He had the audacity to mistaken her for his mammy. Just imagine, he reached for her teats – after all, he had not been weaned but so long ago. But Gipsy, never having had puppies of her own, was embarrassed and shocked. She jumped straight up in the air and let out a yelp of surprise. SPORT looked at her innocently and puzzled, not understanding why she acted so prissy. Well, SPORT, this was the first of a long string of mischievous acts to follow. Anyway, no matter how naughty this little fellow behaved in his youthful naiveté, SPORT and Gipsy were to become best of friends over time.

After their initial few disagreements about SPORT's toys or Gipsy's milk bar, they came around to be really fond of each other. Whenever SPORT was outside the house and Gipsy happened to be in the barbershop downstairs, she came to greet him. They bumped noses, sniffed all over each other's faces and body, and then a wild chase began. They would blitz along the sidewalk, shoulder to shoulder, ears flying, speeding up to the curb, pushing on their breaks to come to a screeching halt just in time before they reached the border stone, then turning around for a race to the other end of the block, where another side street was cutting the walkway. This went on for several times, to and forth, to and forth. *"Yap, yap, yap."* People would leap to the side so that these crazy canines would not bump into them. Some threw their hands over their eyes out of fear that the dogs might run into the street, which they never did. They were simply wild, having immense fun storming up and down the sidewalk until they – very much out of breath – had enough, going into the barber shop and sharing a slurp of water out of Gipsy's dish, which was always waiting there in the back.

The Irish Wolfhound

At other times when we were checking out some of SPORT's traps in a nearby avenue, we occasionally ran into an Irish Wolfhound having his walk out there too. SPORT was in awe, as this dog was almost the size of a pony. SPORT was too leery to greet it. Besides, he would not have even been able to reach up to the dog's belly with his nose. SPORT, probably thinking '*better be safe than sorry*', moved to the other side of me, trying to keep a healthy distance and have someone blocking this giant-sized dog off. SPORT had no reason to be worried, though, as it was a girl dog, not having any intentions to bother him at all. As a matter of fact, we learned later on how gentle and shy this dog really was.

We happened to be in the waiting room of our veterinarian. This giant high-legged dog came in, looking really scared, trying to crawl and sit on the lap of her owner. It appeared to be comical, but in reality it was so touching, as she tried to seek protection in climbing up (or better down) to position herself. But it was not funny to the dog at all, and her owner fondly rubbed and petted her while talking in a soothing voice and eventually being able to calm her fear. It doesn't matter whether a dog is big or small; most of them have made an unpleasant experience of one kind or another with a vet at some time during their life and therefore deeply resent being taken to a vet's office.

The Mongrel

At this same alley where we ran into the Irish Wolfhound, most of the other dog owners in the neighborhood used to meet and walk their pets. Usually, the dogs would be friendly and greet each other, play a while and make their desired social contacts.

But there was this one real strong and aggressive male mongrel that did not tolerate any other male in this vicinity. He looked at this walkway as his personal property, which should be off-limits to anything moving and which he had to defend against any intruder. And every dog he saw was an intruder in his eyes. His owner could hardly hold him when another dog tried to pass by him. This dog hated SPORT. He would almost flip out tearing at his leash, growling and snarling. But SPORT was no wimp and he would snarl back and wildly try to leap at this dog, only being stopped by my very tight grip on his collar. The mere sight of each other aggravated both dogs.

The owner of this hostile dog was cooperative, though. As we usually entered the alley from the opposite ends, we had the unspoken understanding that the one who saw the other one first would turn around and walk instead through an adjacent street. It was not necessary to have the dogs explode in anger, especially as this big mongrel could have easily eaten SPORT alive.

The German Shepherd

SPORT and I happened to be in another unpleasant situation. We were walking in this pretty small park area with a nice lawn and different kinds of bushes in the middle. All of a sudden a big mean-looking German Shepherd came sprinting toward SPORT. Oh Lord, this looked like an upcoming fight, which SPORT and I would more than likely not be able to win. The owner of the Shepherd was still far away, trying to call his dog, but without success. SPORT recognized the danger and calmly moved right into the middle of this garden-bed of low-cut rosebushes. The bushes were cut in such a way that a middle-sized dog like SPORT could still move around easily, but there was no room for the bigger and heavier Shepherd who would have hurt himself, as the stiff branches of these low-cut and narrowly set bushes were in his way.

The Shepherd was pacing around the roundel, snarling, trying to find a path to get to SPORT, who understood very well that the rose bushes were protecting him. So he stayed cool and remained right there where he was, however suspiciously watching every move the Shepherd made. Meanwhile I was trying to get in between both dogs, grabbing a stick to drive the assailant off. But that was not necessary any more, as the owner of the Shepherd had finally arrived, taking over. While SPORT and I - still upset and shaking - walked off to some friendlier place, the other dog was shouted at and brutally beaten up by his owner with his leash. Observing this, I began to feel sorry for this dog although he had behaved aggressively. I just don't believe in beating a dog for punishment like this. There are other ways to train your dog and they have to start at an early age. This poor Shepherd had no choice but to develop into a neurotic and unpredictable creature, having an owner like that!

The SUV

During some other excursions, we walked through this green strip dividing a street. There were several cars parked at the side, one of which was an SUV. Passing by, it suddenly seemed to explode. Some dogs happened to be inside of it and they were trying to defend their territory, barking hysterically at poor little SPORT and me. They jumped and bumped violently at the side windows and snarled and growled, the SUV was shaking and swaying. It was scary, as the dogs were quite big, looking like a Doberman, a Shepherd and some kind of a huge heavy mongrel. No chance that we could have won a fight against them. But they were locked inside and could not get out and do anything else but let out their frustration in throwing a tantrum inside the SUV. So SPORT and I kept on with our walk, a little faster than usually, though, disregarding the uncomfortable feeling of the adrenaline rush, which had made our hair stand up.

About a week later – I had all forgotten about the incident – we happened to walk again in the same neighborhood. There was this same SUV parked at the side again, the three dogs inside. And again, there was no owner to be seen anywhere near. The dogs saw us first, we were still a little distance away. They immediately started to act up, jumping wildly at the windows. I decided to take SPORT to the other side of the street away from this in order not to aggravate them any further.

But it was already too late, because this time their furious bumping into the side windows had an unexpected result, one window busted out with its frame. One of the dogs fell out with it and was now standing there, being totally perplexed. The other two dogs were still inside, looking bewildered. There was a sudden and uneasy silence as all of them had stopped barking. They did not make a move to chase after SPORT, who had meanwhile become invisible standing in the entrance of a front yard across the street. This was a crazy situation, totally unforeseen. The dogs did not have a barrier any more between themselves and us, standing in open space not being their assigned territory, so they suddenly seemed not to know anymore what to do. But before they could change their minds, SPORT and I saw to it that we got away as fast and as far as we could. Turning around and before disappearing into a side street, I still noticed from the distance that the third dog had jumped back into its van again. We decided to avoid this part of the neighborhood for a while during our walks!

Species of a different Kind

Cats

It was a beautiful fresh morning when SPORT – still quite young at that time – and I were walking in the neighborhood along some of the front gardens. SPORT took his time, sniffing at every flower protruding through the fences. He loved the smell of flowers. Then his eyes caught something exciting. A cat had just stepped from behind a bush, hissing at SPORT, slamming her tail to and forth. SPORT was still too naïve to be warned by that and curiously he rushed through the open gate to take a closer look. I called him back, but he had already made the cat retreat to a corner of the house. With her back to the wall, the cat raised up on her hind legs, fur all fluffed up to make herself seem bigger than she really was, hissing furiously and wildly smacking at SPORT with her claw-armored paws, barely missing him. SPORT still did not move away, instead turned around, giving me this look as if to say, *"What is this, why is she acting so strangely?"* I ordered him in no uncertain terms to take his fuzzy little butt out of there immediately! He was just plain lucky that the cat had not ripped him to pieces yet. He came out reluctantly, and while walking away, he glanced at the cat again, still not understanding, why she had turned him away so fiercely. After all, he just would have liked to bite her!

On the way back home we had to pass by the same front garden again, so I put him on the leash just to be on the safe side. He had not forgotten about his little encounter, but still insisted on having another close look through the fence and perhaps giving his newfound "friend" a few barks in retaliation. He was pulling hard at the leash. Good thing I did not allow him to get too close, because right out of the blue the cat ripped through the fence trying to slash her claws at SPORT's face. He was lucky again and got away unscathed. But he still had to go a long way to learn about the facts of life.

During his early months of maturing, SPORT had an occasional fallback from his training, especially when his hunting instinct got the better of him. One day we were walking through a street in the neighborhood, which we called "cat alley" because of the many cats living there. That day I didn't see any of those cats. But that's only because I am a dull human. SPORT soon spotted one of the felines hiding under a car. When he went to investigate, the cat took off. SPORT, watery at the mouth, forgetting everything around him, sprinted after her – *"yap, yap, I'm gonna get ya, I'm gonna get ya"*. They blitzed across the street, barely missed by a screeching car. My heart was at a standstill while they were in a wild pursuit in the backyards of the houses across the street. I couldn't see too much because it was early in the evening and already getting darker. The only thing I could hear was some remote rustling and rumbling and an occasional *"yap, yap, yap"*. *"My goodness, SPORT, we are going to have some words when you come back!"*

And there he came, appearing from behind a garage. He stopped, looking at me, standing there wide-legged, macho-pose, and a wide grin on his face, *"was I good, or was I good"* he seemed to be saying. I didn't hesitate too long, I grabbed him in the neck, scolding him madly. *"You almost got run over by a car, you fool, what has gotten into you? We are going to cut your walk short tonight and will go home right now!"*

SPORT had expected an approval of his action, but instead he was being reprimanded. His ears flapped down, he looked horribly guilty. He walked extra close at my side, not leaving an eye off me, nudging me from time to time as if to say, *"come on, be good again with me"*. It was terribly hard not to give in so soon – because in reality I was so relieved that he had come out of this without a scratch – but he had to understand that he had been doing a no-no. This was the first and only time that I ever had to grab him in the neck, and I never ever wanted to have to do that again.

So, keeping him on the leash more often during our future walks was part of the lesson that we both learned.

When we arrived home and walked into the house, he immediately rushed into his sanctuary, his doghouse, and sat upright deep in the back of it, ears down and lower jaw and lip slightly pushed forward, watching every move that was going on outside his hut. George noticed that something had gone wrong. *"Hey, Sport, did you two have an argument? Have you been a bad boy and did she scold you? I guess, next time you will know better."* We let him sulk a little while, but then we could not bear it any longer ourselves. We talked to him, trying to get him to come out of his house. Reluctantly and very carefully he finally came tiptoeing to us, and we reassured him that he was still the best thing that we had.

Horses

Part of the extended territory of SPORT was the so-called green belt circling the entire city area. Sometimes, mounted police patrolled this region. SPORT was absolutely at awe watching them trot by on their horses. Were these perhaps some giant-sized dogs? No, they couldn't be, they smelled too different. And what dog would carry such strangely dressed human on his back? And the clubbing noise they made walking on the stone-plastered walkway! No, dogs had different feet! *"Sport, these are horses,"* George explained. SPORT preferred to stare from a safe distance, wondering. Then, when one of the horses left a souvenir behind, SPORT raced over to it, carefully sniffing what this steaming something could be. The message clearly was: *"No dog."* Any time later, when SPORT located one of those souvenirs without any horses around, he used to give us this meaningful look, *"see, they were here again."*

Tasty Creatures!

On our excursions through the big park, we found an area that was taken over by a colony of rabbits. They used to be out on the grass early in the morning or later in the evening when there were only a few people around. SPORT knew this and he tried every trick in the world to make us take him over there. Arriving at their terrain, he looked at us, then into the direction of these tasty looking creatures, then made a few steps toward them, stopped, looking at us again, pointing his head over to his intended prey once more. Was he trying to get us to hunt in a pack, as his ancestors used to do out in the wild? His instincts seemed to be taking over. At an occasion like this, SPORT used to get real quiet, duck down a little bit, carefully stalking toward the rabbits. And as soon as he got close enough and one of the rabbits made a move as if to run, he took off into a frantic chase. *"Yap, yap, yap"*. There was no calling him back, he would simply not listen. *"Yap, yap, yap"*. The rabbit, trying to shed its pursuant, zigzagged down under into the bushes, SPORT right behind. *"Yap, yap, yap, yap"*. The rabbits seemed to know what they were doing and seemed to be quite sure that SPORT would not be able to catch any of them. And – SPORT forgive us – we believed the same, after all, SPORT was a spoiled city dog and not a trained hunter, although hunting is part of every dog's nature.

The rabbits seemed to be teasing him. SPORT was having a ball anyway and it took an eternity for him to reappear, being out of breath, empty-mouthed, but totally happy and content with himself. *"Come on SPORT, let's go home. This was enough excitement for today."* I secretly vowed to myself, not to take SPORT to this side of the park anymore, at least not at a time when the rabbits would be out there. I was a party-pooper, I did not want to have a poaching dog. And besides, a main road with speeding cars encircled this area. If any rabbit in its attempt to escape had run into this street, SPORT would have been a goner.

However, SPORT did manage to lure us again a few more times to his beloved hunting grounds. And then the day arrived, when we had to realize that we had underestimated our sweet, cuddly and innocent city dog. That was when SPORT finally came out of the bushes carrying one of the rabbits in his mouth, already dead. SPORT dropped the rabbit at George's feet, expecting to be complimented for his skills. But what did George do? Party pooper! He picked up the rabbit and dropped it into the nearest trash bin! *"What are you doing?"* SPORT was upset. He raced to the trash bin, stood up at it, unsuccessfully trying to reach the rabbit. *"Peep, peep! Why? It was supposed to be our supper! You don't understand! Peep, peep, peeeep!"* SPORT was crying and protesting all the way home.

On one hand, we understood SPORT's joy in chasing and catching and his excitement over this, after all it was the nature of the beast. It hurt us to see SPORT being so disappointed and not letting him have his way anymore, but we were living in the city and could not let him develop any further in this direction. In the future we would try not to have him tempted anymore.

Bushy Tails

We spent a lot of time in the park as a recreation area. Besides of all the dogs that SPORT loved to play with, he occasionally ran upon some other strange creatures that were still alien to him. We were resting under a group of trees away from the sun, when SPORT heard something rustling above. He jumped up, trying to see what that was. There was something reddish brown racing down the big tree trunk, stopping in intervals, lifting its head and glancing around, slipping to the other side of the stem and reappearing again on the front side, all in very elegant and smooth movements. SPORT was puzzled. What was this? He had never seen such a slender, agile creature, having a bushy tail like that, with which it seemed to keep its balance so gracefully. Could he perhaps catch and eat it? *"SPORT, don't even think about it!"* SPORT moved closer to the tree with this interesting prey. The squirrel gave him a bored look, *"what do you want, you couldn't catch me if you tried."* It seemed to ignore SPORT, came down from the tree and – in utter disrespect – moved on rather close to us, gathering some acorns. SPORT was fascinated, inching toward the squirrel. He would have loved to get a close sniff – or more – of it. But the squirrel kept disregarding him, went about its business of collecting food and eventually moved back up the tree and disappeared.

SPORT had many more encounters with other squirrels at later times. He could never get as close to them as he might have liked and he finally seemed to accept the fact that he would never have the chance to catch any of them. So he usually just stood there captivated, watching them in amazement.

Flying Insects

There were other creatures that did not exactly amaze SPORT, but severely annoyed him. Those were flies. Whenever one of those big shimmering buzzers happened to come into the house, SPORT would totally flip out. He would spurt after it, lunge and snap at it. He tried to focus on this disgusting thing, looking around, and then losing sight of it, just when the buzz was coming from another corner of the room. It made him hysterical. One of these insects must have tried to land on SPORT at some time before, because he would keep biting and picking on his fur all over after he had seen one of them, reminding me of ourselves when the mere thought of a flea would make us scratch all over. After SPORT had learned that George used a fly swat, the little smart guy would come running to us to incorporate our help in chasing the fly outside or squash it.

We could understand SPORT very well in his aversion against flies, but we had to be watchful that he would not also chase other flying insects, such as bees, wasps or bumblebees, because these were of a somewhat different kind and able to possibly sting him. Exactly this happened one day in the park. He had been running across a patch of clover and suddenly cried out loud, holding his right front foot up, wailing. We rushed over to him to see what happened. We could not see anything at his foot like a splinter or a thorn, but we found a squirming bee lying in the grass where SPORT was standing. So that's what it was. He had stepped on a bee and the bee had stung him. SPORT frantically licked at the pads of his paw, trying to soothe the pain. While the paw began to swell slightly, we took him home immediately. A patch soaked in a vinegar-mixture was wrapped around his foot, held by a baby sock so that SPORT would not remove the remedy.

After the first shock, SPORT took this event lightly, though. He settled down in his "nest" at home and enjoyed the fuss being made over him. The next day, his paw looked all normal and he walked around just as if nothing had happened. The bee sting affected him less than I could remember it affecting me as a child. "*Ok, SPORT, we know you are a toughie!*"

The Feathered Species

Beside the four-legged and the buzzing fellow-creatures, SPORT had yet to meet the feathered kind. Of course he had seen some birds around, especially the many pigeons in the neighborhood. But somehow he had never bothered much about them. Now George was taking him along to this little lake nearby, where a lot of ducks had made their home. George sometimes liked to feed them with leftover bread. Whenever George appeared, the ducks came streaming by. SPORT watched this with real interest, perhaps not exactly with a noble ulterior motive. But if ever a chase might have crossed his mind, George stopped him. SPORT learned quickly that he was not to disturb these quacking, waddling friends, who first were a bit reluctant, when they saw SPORT eyeing them. But SPORT behaved well and never stirred them up as some other dogs sometimes tried. So, George and SPORT both enjoyed some tranquil afternoons at the lake watching the ducks battling over the best pieces of bread, then swim away again, rippling the water while diving under or grooming their feathers.

Man out of Space?

And there was yet another species of a different kind that SPORT had never seen before. This was no species of the animal world, but although it was from the human family, it must have seemed to SPORT as being from another planet. This was the time shortly after the beginning of the Gulf war. All the American military installations – there were several in our region - were specially secured. One of these installations – a housing area of single officers – was in our extended neighborhood and we used to pass by there on the way to our beloved large park. By then, rolls of barbed wire surrounded this housing area and sometimes a patrolling guard was seen.

On this particular day, a guard was standing there, blocking the only opening of the barbed wire barrier. We were still quite some distance away, but SPORT took this opportunity and raced over to the guy, placed himself in front of him, looking him up and down, then walked half-way around him and back again, just a-looking. He was just too curious of this figure, which was standing there wide-legged and in full gear, heavy boots, helmet on his head decorated with some sort of camouflage, backpack and all kind of things of who-knows-what strapped to his green and brown shaded fatigues. And holding a rifle under his arm, pointed to the ground, didn't exactly make this stern-faced guy more trustworthy.

Although I did not seriously believe that the soldier would shoot at SPORT, it still gave me the creeps seeing the rifle and at the same time SPORT messing with the guy. I called him off. But SPORT insisted on staring some more. He had never seen anything like this, was it a man out of space? He sat down in front of the guy, bent his head somewhat to the side and just kept looking him up and down.

Now the guard could not keep his stern expression any longer, he began to chuckle and then broke out laughing. *"This is some cute dog you have, ma'am. What is it, a Schnauzer?" "Yes",* I replied, *"and a darned hard headed one at that. Sorry if he bothered you." "That's okay. I just know now that I will get me the same kind of dog once I am back home again."* Come on SPORT, you charmer, you did it again!

Neighbors and Visitors

After SPORT had just come to live at our home, he did not yet know all the other people living in the building. That meant that SPORT would bark at any person walking past our apartment door. He used to sniff at the crack under the door to get the scent of whoever it was. So in time, he was able to identify who belonged in the house and who did not, and he stopped the barking.

Teasing Neighbors

But then there were those two young guys, living on the top floor. They could not withstand giving SPORT a few barks back in return. Every time they passed by our door, they would go *"woof, woof, Sport, woof!"* This never failed to make SPORT go berserk. He did not like to be teased. And whenever they happened to meet outside, SPORT ran up to them, growling madly, his hair all fluffed up *"Don't you mess with me again, I am the big bad Wolf"!* But he would never attack or bite. When those guys then tried to talk, joke or play with him, he would ignore that. He simply never wanted to be friends with them.

Secret Love

The situation was quite the opposite with another neighbor. George and SPORT used to run into her when they were coming back home from their early morning walk and she was just coming down the stairs on her way to work. They always exchanged a few jokes and friendly words, and SPORT got around to liking her, more than any of the other neighbors, who usually also had something nice to say to SPORT. If we happened to meet outside, SPORT would happily run over to her and revel in the attention, stroking units and sweet talk she would give him. Sometimes he was so starry-eyed that he would follow behind her although she was going in a different direction than we were, and we had to call him back. It seemed that SPORT had a secret love. But he was making it all so obvious!

Workmen

SPORT, in general, was a friendly dog. But whenever a stranger came to the door, he let him know that this was his territory. If a workman needed to get in, we first had to assure SPORT that this was okay and call him back, before he stopped his barking. Then, when this person opened his tool kit, SPORT was all over it, curiously checking what this was about. The guys usually did not mind and all of them gave SPORT some attention, but we did not want him to be in the way or even accidentally get hurt or hinder the guy in his job, so we ordered him to get away. Then SPORT would place himself somewhere else in the room, picking a strategic point where he could keep an eye on the person, watching every move he made. And when the work was finished, SPORT would follow and escort the guy to the door.

Unwanted Intruders

Sometimes the front door of the house had been left open and people came in who had no business there. That was the time when SPORT became the big protector. One day a strange person rang our doorbell, standing already right in front of our apartment door, wanting to collect charity money, but showing no ID. As SPORT was loudly protesting, this person demanded in a very harsh tone to remove the dog. *"Why, this dog lives here, you don't. And we did not ask you to come into this building either."* This settled the case and the person left grumbling.

At another time, the front door of the house was open again, someone had rung the bell from downstairs and was now coming up. I did not know him, he was looking dubious and I asked him what he wanted. *"Um, eh... I want.. eh..."*. He did not get far because SPORT had by now run down the stairs to see who that was. Although SPORT had stopped barking when we started to talk, he now sniffed at the guy, growling mildly. And the guy froze, he seemed somewhat anxious, raising his arms a bit, *"Is this your dog?" "Yes, this is my dog,"* I answered, while SPORT now moved on past the guy, walking through the open front door, lifting his leg at the corner of the house and thus demonstrating that this was his territory.

The guy now seemed to be at a loss of what to do. He had stopped halfway in the stairwell. Upstairs, I was blocking the way and SPORT, who might – in the guy's mind – perhaps bite him, was standing downstairs. Well, to put an end to this situation, I called SPORT back in. And then I really had to grin, because as soon as SPORT came back into the house to get upstairs and had passed by the stranger again, the guy uttered real quickly, *"Um, eh... I have just changed my mind, I don't really want anything"* and off he was, faster than you could blink. I was sure that this person had come into our house with no-good intentions, that he wanted to case the place or else. So SPORT had evidently scared the man away. Good so, SPORT was beginning to earn his livelihood.

Occasionally, when visitors for any of the other tenants in the house happened to walk upstairs, SPORT ran to the front door of the apartment, holding up his head slightly tilted and turning his ears to get the best position for the best sound. And he would sniff at the crack under the door to get a good whiff. If he did not approve of the people, he would make sure that they did not stop at our door. His hair rising, he would let out his deepest and most dangerous growl, trying to sound like the big bad wolf. You would not believe that a middle-sized Schnauzer could produce sounds complimentary to a heavy wide-chested Rottweiler. Anyone who did not know SPORT had to believe that a giant monster was hovering behind the door. So we were quite at ease if we had to leave SPORT alone at home. He was capable of scaring away any unwanted person.

Every Dog's special Friend

And like for most dogs, there was this one very special person. During the nice-weather seasons, SPORT had his favorite place on our front balcony, overlooking the street and the side of our house. There he used to sit comfortably on a bench, resting his head on the railing, watching everything going on outside. The peace was suddenly interrupted, when a person came pushing his cart around the corner, steering toward our mailboxes. SPORT began to raise hell, letting us know that the mailman had arrived. Of course, being a dog, SPORT had a special relationship with the mailman. It is hard to understand, though, why most dogs are so aggressive to mailmen, who normally are all nice people, just doing their job. Perhaps because they have to fumble with other people's property, the mailbox.

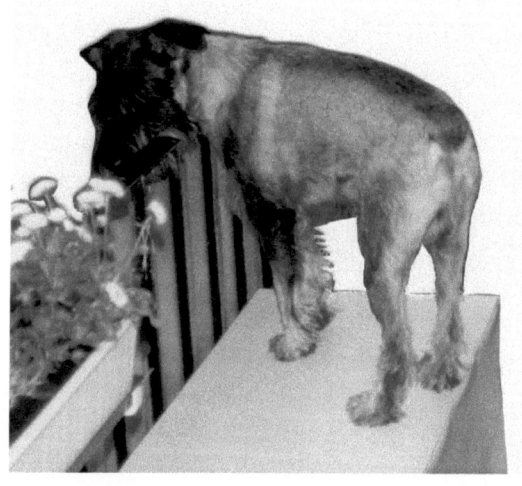

But that alone could not be it, because if we happened to run into our or any other mailman away from the house just pushing his cart, SPORT would still get angry and growl at him. Luckily, our mailman did not take SPORT's naughty behavior personal or in any way upsetting, in fact, he used to call on him, *"Come on, SPORT, you should know me by now!"* But SPORT decided to keep on being impossible.

Friends of the House

Any visitor to the house that we approved of would normally be greeted by SPORT in a friendly and rather curious way. After his first inspection of the person, SPORT would go and find one of his toys to bring and drop it at the visitor's feet. This usually earned him a few stroking units, and he was happy.

If we had several friends over and the evening was filled with music, laughter and discussions, SPORT was normally right in the middle of it. But then, if the evening got longer and by late there was still some commotion going on, SPORT could get kind of annoyed. First he would retreat to his bunk in the back room, but after a while he reappeared where the crowd was, looking around, then looking at George or me, then again at the crowd. Sometimes he would snap the air in their direction. After two or three repeats of this demonstration, it was embarrassingly obvious that he wanted them to leave.

In a situation like this, I usually grabbed SPORT, picked him up and carried him back into the other room, smooching with him, trying to tuck him in, and talk to him for some time while rubbing and stroking him. He enjoyed this and sometimes, if I was lucky, he went to sleep and stayed on his bunk.

SPORT was absolutely crazy about two of our friends. If Dee or Charlie came by, SPORT would greet them, dancing around their feet, jumping up at their legs and making them do what he loved the most, having them chase him around the house. They did this willingly, having a ball themselves this way. After this initial phase, all of them settled down. SPORT would lay down somewhere nearby, head resting on his forefeet. He listened to the conversation going on, and although his eyes were covered by his long brows, one could still notice his eyes moving from person to person because his extra-long eyelashes were moving along with them, thus causing the eyebrows to slightly ruffle. SPORT loved the company of these friends because they were giving him all the attention he wanted. As far as he was concerned, they belonged to the pack.

But there was this other acquaintance who was a little uneasy around our dog and did not quite know how to react when SPORT came to greet him or just stood there looking at him. He had the tendency to ignore SPORT. This really hurt SPORT's feelings. As a puppy, he did not know yet how to deal with this. And this one day, shortly after this friend had arrived at our house, SPORT was missing. Where was he? He had just been sitting there a minute ago. I called him and looked around in every room, but could not find him. Then I finally discovered him. He sat upright far in the back of his doghouse, in his sanctuary, trembling strongly. I thought that he had become sick and tried to make him come out of there so I could see what was wrong with him. It took an eternity for him to come to me. I picked him up, holding him on my arms, soothing and comforting him. There seemed to be nothing wrong with him physically. But why was he so distressed? Then it began to dawn on me that he must have felt left out. We had ignored him too long. Poor little SPORT, we learned that he had a real sensitive soul. An incident like this should not happen again, we were going to look after that. SPORT did not necessarily need to be the center of attention, but he wanted at least to be recognized and be part of the crowd and get some kind of consideration now and then. He deserved this.

After SPORT had become grown and more self-confident, he simply let this same guy – I will give him the name Albert here – know that he should stop being so uptight. It was real funny to see how he went about this. Albert had sat down on our couch and SPORT jumped up right next to him, sitting up straight, looking at him. You could see it in his eyes, he had something mischievous on his mind. Albert cringed, did he sense what was coming? SPORT reached over to him, scratching his arm with his front paw and then – it was hilarious – planted a smooch right on Albert's cheek. Albert's reaction was the same as Lucy of the Peanuts series showed when Snoopy kissed her, he was disgusted. Now, all of this happened so quickly, we almost missed it and could not call SPORT away fast enough, we really did not want SPORT to bother anybody this way. But SPORT did not care, he just had made his point and wanted to be friends with Albert.

Occasionally, Markus the barber would call us on the phone, telling us that he wanted to come by for a few minutes. As SPORT knew Markus, he always greeted him friendly at the door. SPORT's keen ears evidently could identify Markus' voice on the phone, and as soon as the phone rang and it was Markus, SPORT would run to the door, eagerly waiting for him to show up. But sometimes Markus only called to chat and not to visit, and SPORT could not understand why he was not coming up the stairs, after all he had just heard his voice. *"Peep?" "No, Sport, you guessed wrong, Markus will not come up now."* SPORT seemed disappointed but then settled down again on the place where he had been resting before.

Canine Visitors

Our place sometimes looked as if we had a house full of children, for all the toys lying around. We regularly gathered them up and put them on top of SPORT's doghouse. Which was okay with SPORT, because he always knew where to find them. Other guests, especially the four-legged ones, seemed to appreciate this too, as they would be walking straight to SPORT's house and grab one of his squeakers or a ball. SPORT did not like this at all, depending on the visitor, but many times he just played and wrestled together with his visiting friends.

Now and then, Monty, the Westhighland Terrier, came by with his owner, my friend Gaby. While she and I were sitting there chatting, something was going on between SPORT and Monty. SPORT knew that I had a soft spot for Monty, so he was not particularly fond of him, he just tolerated him. Monty was going on excursion through the house with SPORT following right behind him, watching every step of him suspiciously. But Monty was a nice guy, who was not about to do anything unruly. So he finally came back in to be with us again. SPORT eyed Monty and made sure that he didn't dare to lie down too close to me, SPORT could be real jealous, especially if the other dog was also a male. He jumped up on the couch next to me, stood up there, demonstratively looking down on Monty, *"Hey, this is my territory, you stay down there and behave. I will be up here overlooking every move you make!"* Now, we all knew that Monty was not a timid dog, he could be quite frisky and boisterous on his own turf and especially outside. But this was not his home, this was strange terrain. He decided to respect SPORT's demand for sovereignty and walked over to his owner, not caring about any muscle flexing of bigheaded SPORT. So Gaby and I ended up sitting there, both of us rubbing our dogs and assuring them that each of them were the greatest and most important in the hearts of their respective owners. You know you have to respect the feelings of your pets!

There was this sad day when Markus had given Gipsy away. He just did not have enough time to take her out regularly and give her all the attention that this sweet dog needed. One of his customers had taken her and she was now living at a great place outside the city. She could roam around in a big house with yard and garden, and a whole family was taking care of her and giving her all the love and attention she deserved. She really blossomed since she had found her new home and had a regular schedule, and she was looking great. Whenever this customer came to the city, she also brought Gipsy along to the shop. Markus would call us up so that SPORT and Gipsy could meet again. If we could not come downstairs, Gipsy would come up to the apartment. It was heartwarming to watch them interact. Despite the animosities of earlier times, they had come to the point where they really liked each other. They stood there chest to chest, looking at one another, their stumpy tails twirling. Then they smooched and rubbed faces, nibbling tenderly at each other's necks and ears. Everyone in the room became quiet, smiling while watching this scene. SPORT and Gipsy ran through the house side by side in close body contact, then started to slide along on the floor, butts up in the air, fronts down and nose to nose, gurgling and cooing like love-stricken doves. They kept going on and on, demonstration their happiness in a most adorable way. After a long while they rested, stretched out on the floor, face to face, just looking at one another. Were there little pink hearts dancing in the air? No wonder that Gipsy was always welcome in our home.

Unexpected furry Visitor

One morning I stepped onto our back balcony to check on our botanical friends. But what was this? Something jumped up and fled, hiding behind one of the large flowerpots. I went to investigate and came to look into a pair of fearfully widened green eyes, staring at me out of a face lined with black and gray stripes and with long dark whiskers next to a pink-colored triangle of a nose. *"Well, look at this. How in the world did you get up here?"* I spoke softly to this unexpected feline visitor, not wanting to frighten her any further. What had made her get up here? It seemed impossible, as it was not a ground floor apartment but the next flight upstairs. Perhaps she had been in a wild chase on the roofs of some of the garages below and had jumped from there onto our balcony in a giant leap to save herself from some vicious pursuer. And then, when she found herself in this strange and fenced-in environment did not know anymore how to get out of it again. She must have stayed here all night, scared out of her wits.

She was not defensive or aggressive at all, instead she fearfully opened her mouth and gave off a pitiful *"meeooow"*. *"Come on, pretty thing, don't be afraid, I will take you out of here so you can go home"*, I tried to soothe her. But there was a problem – SPORT was inside! Therefore I could not just walk with her through our place, perhaps giving her some water to drink and a bite to eat before letting her out at the front door - SPORT would very jealously defend his territory and try to tear the strange cat to pieces. So I called on George to take SPORT and have him restricted to the back room and close the door behind him for a few minutes because I had this cat to carry through the house. Of course George was confused, wanting to know what the hell was going on – restricting his dog to the back room! And what cat anyway? *"Don't ask, just do, I'll explain later"*, I let him know. Grudgingly George did as I said while I was coaxing the cat to come to me so that I could pick her up and carry her to her freedom.

Sweet thing, holding her on my arms I wished that I could keep her, as I was still a cat lover deep down inside. But she was not mine and surely I would never betray SPORT this way. So, kitty had to go. With some comforting words and a few stroking units I released her at the front door and happily she took off to wherever her home was. While I was explaining to George what happened, SPORT put his antenna up, snooping around, sensing our short-time feline visitor. How this cat had made it to our balcony will forever remain her secret.

Visiting Other People's House

Monty's Home

This one afternoon, SPORT and I were on our way to visit my friend Gaby in the neighborhood. This was a first for SPORT, and at the entrance to her house and in the elevator, SPORT began sniffing around intensely, *"Sniff, sniff, interesting, I know this smell! Sniff, sniff, yes, there must be Monty somewhere around!"* When we arrived at Gaby's door, Monty was already barking behind the door, expecting the visitors. After the greeting ritual of SPORT and Monty, SPORT went immediately investigating the whole house, Monty right in his tracks and watching him skeptically. After all, this time SPORT was the visitor and here was Monty-territory. So far, he did not complain, but when SPORT detected Monty's food dish and was brazing enough to start munching on some leftovers, Monty protested and barked at SPORT. I rushed over to the scene and with a sharp "*no*" addressed to SPORT, I took Monty's dish and put it out of reach. In order to take their attention away from Monty's bowl, both dogs were given a treat. After that, SPORT and Monty settled down in some distance from each other, but closely eyeing the other, full of suspicion. They were not enemies, but they also never really became friends either. Perhaps because both were males and, at best, would only tolerate one another.

Charlie's Cat

There was another place, to which SPORT accompanied George when he was out visiting friends. This home belonged to Inge and Charlie, two of those friends whom SPORT really liked. But this place was also residence to Timmy, a big and real misgiving tomcat. That is, he was only misgiving to SPORT. As soon as Timmy eyed SPORT, his fur would fluff up, and wildly hissing at him he tried to keep our greedy dog away from the kitchen. This was understandable, as SPORT had discovered that Timmy's food dish was placed in there and he usually went straight into that direction. SPORT ignored Timmy totally, as cat food seemed irresistible to him. While he was plundering Timmy's dish, the cat had retreated on top of a cabinet, watching him from up there full of hostility.

In order to avoid any further aggravation when SPORT came to visit in the future, Timmy's food dish was then moved to a higher place where SPORT could not reach it. SPORT had created himself a mortal enemy through his greediness.

At a neighbor's house

There was a neighbor whom SPORT also was very fond of. She lived right across the street from us and always had a few nice words to say to SPORT or rubbed his head. As she had offered several times that she would like to take care of him if ever we wanted to go someplace where SPORT could not come with us, we let her have him one evening when we went out to town.

SPORT liked it over in her apartment and comfortably settled down, he even seemed not to care when we were ready to go and leave him behind. He didn't even make a move to get up to see us to the door. But when we called up our neighbor later in the evening to see how our dog was doing, she explained that he was sweet and calm during the first few hours, but then he became uneasy and wanted to leave her place. He had come several times to her, *woofed* and then walked to the door, staring at the handle. As she was not to let him out, SPORT settled down again, but began to whine. *Where are my people? Why do they stay away for so long?* He was missing his familiar pack.

When George and I came back home late that evening, SPORT was happy, but let us know that we were not to do this again to him. Evidently he did not take it so good to be with someone else alone at a different place without any of us being present, even though he really liked this particular person. This was our fault, as he had always been with either one or both of us. He was just too fixated on us alone. This also showed in the fact that he would refuse to go for a walk with anyone but us. On one hand this was positive, because he could not be stolen so easy, but on the other hand it tied us down because we could not take him with us everywhere and he could not be left alone at home for too long.

The Home Buddy

Alone at Home

Although we used to take SPORT with us whenever and wherever this was possible, there were times when we had to leave him alone at home. SPORT of course would have always preferred to accompany us when we had to go outside, but he normally did not make much trouble if he had to stay behind. Naturally he came running immediately if he heard us getting ready,

watching us with this hopeful expression on his face, stumpy tail twirling. Then when it dawned on him that he was to stay at home, he gave us this disappointed guilt-producing look and he would turn around and walk into the other room, head and ears down. He would simply lie down at one of his favorite spots and take a nap. He never tore up anything in the house out of frustration or loneliness, howling and stirring up the whole neighborhood. SPORT just seemed to feel at ease at home. He had learned early that we would always come back to him soon. He could definitely be sure of that because we loved him dearly and we would never leave him alone too long.

Bringing a Surprise

Then, when we finally came back home, we could hear him already waiting behind the door, whining with excitement, while we put the key in the lock opening the door. SPORT would greet us happily and then immediately investigate any bags we were carrying. Our curious dog had to know what was in there, perhaps a toy or some of his preferred dog treats? He knew that occasionally we came home with a surprise for him. If he snooped around in the bag and found a pack of those tasty dog sticks or even a "bone" made from buffalo hide, he couldn't be stopped. He grabbed the goody, raced through the house, throwing the stick or bone high in the air and catching it again. Or let it be his absolute favorite – a roasted pig ear, SPORT would be squealing and yapping and parading around with it. Then he carried his treasure to the same little old throw rug, which he had chosen as his favorite spot to settle down on during such occasions and then savor on the treat, holding it between his front paws, sniffing, licking and gnawing on it. He was in seventh heaven.

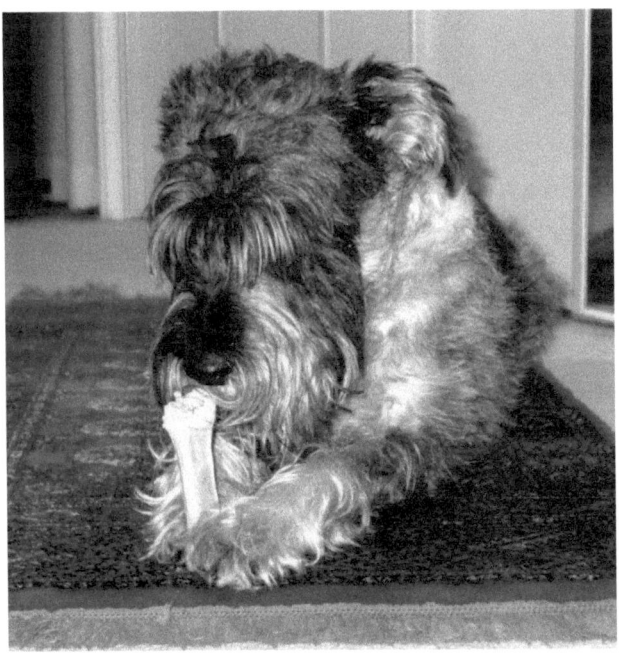

If the surprise happened to be a toy, he was just as delighted. SPORT loved to own things. He would take the gadget in his mouth, chew and smack on it, making it squeak or chase it around on the floor, lift it up and hold it in his mouth toward us, his eyes blinking happily and his stumpy tail twirling. And sometimes he nudged us with his paw, *"look what I've got."* It was fun watching him express his joy.

Imaginary Rabbits

One day I came home from shopping, proudly showing George a pair of fluffy house slippers that I had bought for myself. When SPORT saw this, he ran up to us, jumped at one of the slippers, snatched it away from my hand and took off into the other room to his sanctuary. SPORT must have thought that this furry house slipper was supposed to be for him to play with. My fault, because most of the times I brought something home for him, only on this particular day I had not. He would not voluntarily give the slipper up again and grumbled at me while I was trying to take it away from him. But if I ever thought that I would have any peace wearing my new house slippers, I was seriously wrong. Whenever I dared to walk around the house in my slippers, a raving monster would be attacking my feet. I shouted at SPORT, I pushed him away, nothing helped. He had declared these slippers to be his and only his and was not going to share them. He grabbed and pulled at them until he got one of them off my feet and then ran, proudly carrying his loot, shaking it wildly as he might have done with some wild prey. It seemed as if these slippers had mutated into some imaginary rabbits for SPORT, who had a ball ravaging them.

Eventually, I became tired of this "game", especially after the slippers began to look real battered. SPORT had won, I gave up my house slippers. We kept playing with them, though, until they looked just too torn. And one day, when SPORT was not around, I did the unthinkable and threw them into our trash bin, believing that this story was now over. But this could not have been farther from reality. SPORT was back in the house and he had detected one of the slippers still sticking in the wastebasket before we had taken it out. He ran to me, *"peep, peep"* and led me to the site of crime. With big begging eyes he looked at me, well aware that he was not allowed to snoop around in the trash, not to talk about sneaking something out of it. *"SPORT, you caught me"*, I admitted with a bad conscience, *"You are serious about those darned things, are you?"* His hopeful *"peep, peep!"* and his wiggling stumpy tail never failed to convince me. *"Well, I guess we can live a little longer with this ugly thing if you insist or if your heart is going to break otherwise."* I picked the old slipper back out of the wastebasket and SPORT happily ran off with it. He had won again.

Playthings

As we regularly collected his playthings from all over the apartment and placed them on top of his doghouse, SPORT would always know where to find them. He used to stand up against his hut on his hind legs and then reach with his mouth for whatever he wanted to play with. SPORT had several items that he preferred over the others and when he was ready for a game, he would bring any one of them to us for some action. We would wrestle over a toy, throw it for him to fetch, or hide it so he would have to search for it, and if he found it, SPORT was the proudest fellow around.

SPORT loved these game sessions and did not stop trying to persuade us if we happened not to be in the mood to play. He sometimes got real cocky, jumped up on the roof of his doghouse and started to woof at us, eyes sparkling mischievously. If we did not react to this, he began to throw down his toys from the roof, one after the other, stopping in between to look at us to see how we were taking this. *"Okay you naughty little guy, you got our attention alright, but not the way you hoped for!"* I usually grabbed this misbehaving rascal and simply put him back on the floor, which he most of the times tried to avoid, wig-

gling and squirming. This did not help him much, though. And once back on the floor, he quickly cooled off again, going about some other business.

The Pillow

I had noticed that SPORT liked to lay his head on something slightly higher than the floor when he settled down. Beside his regular blanket, I had already put a small pillow in his hut so that he would have it more comfortable. He began to drag the pillow around with him in the house to rest his head on it. This pillow was the size of a normal deco sofa pillow and therefore somewhat impractical to tow around. So I took it one day, rolled it up real tight and fitted a sorted-out terry cloth towel around it as a pillowcase. SPORT was enthused, this roll-shaped thing was now the right size for him to grab and carry and it became his constant companion around the house. If we had company, SPORT would bring his newest possession into the room and rest comfortably on it – much to the amusement of our visitors.

From time to time, this pillow became a bit worn, though, from its heavy usage and also because SPORT occasionally gnawed on it. That was the time to repair it, but only under the watchful eyes of an eager SPORT. He was not about to give his treasure up. He would be sitting right next to me, not letting his pillow out of sight, sometimes impatiently grabbing for it while I was stitching it up. *"Good grief, SPORT, you are going to get it back again."* And then, finally, the pillow was done and he could happily stroll into the other room, holding his beloved cushion in his mouth, head high up.

Treasure Hunting

SPORT had a thing about cardboard. If we were tearing up an old carton or a box to be put into the trash, he usually ran up to us, insisting to get a piece of it. Or when he saw us finishing a roll of kitchen towels, SPORT would eagerly grab for the cardboard tube from inside the paper towels. He did not allow us to just throw it into the trash. We sometimes playfully teased him about it, bouncing it on his butt, running away with it, closely chased by a gleeful SPORT. After he had finally captured his desired bounty, and after he had paraded around with it enough, he was then looking for a place to hide it. SPORT was in a dilemma, as there was no way to dig a hole in the house as he could have done outside in a yard. He was stalking around in the living room, trying to find a suitable corner. If he noticed us watching him, he would put on a totally innocent disguise, *"I am not up to anything, who, me?"* So we left him alone, acting as if we did not see anything. Eventually, he found a place to satisfy his requirements for a suitable hiding place. So it came to it that we later found some cardboard sticking out from behind a pillow on our couch, or from behind a flowerpot. Sometimes we detected a piece halfway pinned beneath the corner of a carpet. SPORT had done his best under the circumstances.

But the real funny part began, when SPORT one day came to me, trying to tell me something. What was he up to? He tried to make me follow him. So I got up, walking behind him into the living room. SPORT stopped, just standing there, looking at me. *"What is it SPORT?"* He pointed his head repeatedly to this one corner of the room, then looked harmlessly into the air. When I made a few steps into his aimed direction, SPORT acted excited. He quickly looked at this corner again, then again at me, seemingly innocent. *"Oh, now I realize it, you want to see if I can find one of your secretly stashed-away treasures?"* By that time I had long spied a corner of this piece of cardboard peeking around a pillow on the couch. I played the game. I acted as if I was searching for his hidden treasure, just glancing around. And then, finally, I lifted the pillow and laughed, *"Oh, I found it, I found it."* SPORT was jumping around me, all thrilled about his little plot of hide and seek. From now on, he would always come to see if I could find the item that he had just been hiding. This dog was just too much!

Where is George?

Why in the world would a homo sapiens tease his pet canine? When SPORT was a puppy, I had borrowed a video camera and followed my most favorite target around the house and the park to make a sequence of him and George fooling around. Out came a few cute scenes of both of them, containing also SPORT's thrilled "*woof woofs*" and the voice of George. Years later, as I watched this video over, reveling in earlier times and enjoying SPORT being a puppy once again, SPORT came running from the other room, totally excited, looking around. What was going on, he had just heard George's voice? But he was not here! With question marks all over his face, he looked at the TV-set, then at me. There it was again, George's voice calling his name! *"Woof??"* Very puzzled, SPORT circled the TV-set, snooping around, maybe George was hiding behind it? But no, there was no George! And then something else sounded familiar, a dog's squeaky bark! SPORT stood there, head slightly cocked to the side, trying to figure out what this was all about. It seemed that SPORT did not realize what was shown on the video, only the sounds caught his attention. Then George walked into the room and made SPORT's confusion complete. There was George at one end of the room, but his voice coming from the other end. Was SPORT hallucinating? No, the real George now rubbed his back, talking with his real voice to him. And the voice from the other end of the room was cut off. Enough was enough, no teasing – although unintended – anymore!

Privacy

Having SPORT living with us, there was no privacy any more in our house. He would follow us anywhere anytime. Even our visitors had to be warned to make sure to lock the bathroom door behind them, or they would have to face unwanted company. If any one of us was in the bathroom and had not locked the door, SPORT unfailingly showed up a short time later. First, the door opened up just slightly, almost unnoticeably. Then a shiny black nose appeared between the crack. Having his head tilted a bit, SPORT was trying to peek around the corner to see what was going on in there. It usually made me chuckle. *"Well, SPORT, don't be shy. Come on in."* An amused George called from the back *"Sport, if you dare to go in the bathroom with her in it, then it must be true love!"* But SPORT decided to ignore George and pushed through the door, just standing there, his eyes following every move I made and just watching me put my make-up on and groom myself. *"You want a little color on your nose too?"* I let him sniff at a small dab of make-up on my hand, but this seemed not to turn him on. *"Your nose looks better anyway in its natural black"* I assured him. His very intense and earnest look at me confirmed that he agreed.

Every now and then I woke up cold from my sleep in the middle of the night. Someone seemed to be staring at me. Slowly opening the lid of one eye I saw a low shadow in the door, standing there motionless on four legs, just a looking. *"What is it SPORT,"* I mumbled, *"are you checking that everything is in order?"* It was one of SPORT's habits to sometimes tiptoe through the house at night as if patrolling a beat. Perhaps George or I talked in our sleep, had coughed or even snored, which disturbed our precious friend and he had to look and see whether we were all right.

The Bath Attendant

Another thing SPORT used to watch in awe. He did not understand that we would take a shower or a bath voluntarily, as he himself was not exactly fond of this procedure. However, he was curious enough to bust in the door and see who was splashing there in the bathtub under a mountain of soap bubbles. He would stand up on his hind legs, leaning his front legs on the rim of the tub, sometimes licking at George's arm – not so much as to help him clean up, we assumed, but to get a taste of this strange looking frothy substance. *"You never tasted anything like this before, did you?"* George would ask and dab some foam on SPORT's nose. The bursting bubbles tickled him and made him sneeze. SPORT gave George a surprised look, but he kind of liked this action. He kept standing there for a while, just watching George enjoying his bath. Then he decided that he had done enough of this job as a bath attendant and walked out – *"see you in here next time."*

Is SPORT jealous?

If during such occasions I scrubbed George's back or put some lotion on his back after a shower, SPORT would join us, just standing there and watching us, looking us up and down, trying to understand what we were doing. Now and then he would nudge me, like he wanted to interrupt something that he did not quite approve of. *"Peep!"* Was he jealous? It seemed like it. It was funny to me. There I was between my two men, spoiling one of them and the other one was complaining. While George was enjoying the care given to him, he simply said to SPORT *"get out of here, this is my time with her"*. Then I assured SPORT that it was okay, that his turn was coming also. And as soon as I was finished scrubbing George's back, SPORT was claiming his part of the deal and I would give him an ample amount of stroking units, hugging and smooching him, and his world was in order again.

The Peacemaker

SPORT could get quite confused if George and I were having a disagreement. If we happened to yell at each other – which occurs in every relationship now and then – SPORT would come and stand nearby, looking with wide eyes from one to the other. Sometimes he *"woofed"* at us or even nudged us. He did not like for us to fight at all. He was in a dilemma, on one hand he had this strong loyalty toward George, but then again he was quite protective of me. So it came that SPORT often was the peacemaker between us. When we saw the despair in his eyes, this would make us behave immediately and tune down again. And if we did not want to talk to each other directly, we used SPORT as a medium *"Sport go and tell him (or her) that…."* or similar. SPORT could not repeat what we told him, but the other person always heard what was being said to SPORT, so the message arrived anyway. This sort of indirect communication worked, and we loved SPORT the more for it.

The Couch

In the evenings, SPORT used to go to sleep rather early. His hut in the bedroom was his favorite place for a long time. And sometimes at night, he moved around the house to lie down either in his living room nest or in some corner elsewhere. But eventually, he adopted the couch in the back room. We had put a blanket on one end of it where SPORT used to curl up and snooze. Over time, however, he also selected one of the larger pillows at the other end of the couch to snuggle in and rest comfortably on. This meant that he had silently taken over the whole sofa. And this territory had to be defended! SPORT did not like it at all if anyone wanted to sit on "his" sofa, not to talk about lying down or taking a nap. He barely tolerated this from George or from me – and then only for a short time. He would give us these looks and perhaps a short woof, or he would try in the most charming way to lure us away from there.

And then, what a disaster for SPORT, one day our nephew came to visit and stayed for a while. So we needed this couch in the back room for him to sleep on. SPORT was upset. He became very alert when the sofa was converted into a bed and he immediately jumped up on it to demonstrate *"hey, don't get any false impressions, this place is my territory and I don't like what you are doing!"* But nevertheless, he listened when we ordered him down, praising him for leaving so generously "his" couch to our poor visitor, who by now must have really felt welcome. SPORT had to and did accept this temporary set-up. Our nephew loved dogs and fully understood SPORT's behavior. We gave SPORT some extra attention during this time so that he would not feel too downgraded. However, every now and then SPORT would walk up to the door of the back room in the evenings, staring with silent malice at the occupant of his beloved couch.

Cuddling Time

SPORT had a certain ritual before he went to sleep at night. After he had taken over the couch, we used to peek around the corner when we passed by the back room to see if he was already asleep. Sometimes he was soundly snoring away in his dreams, sometimes he lifted his head to see who was checking on him. Then we usually walked in, smooching and rubbing him, saying good night.

This one evening, George and I were watching TV in the other room, SPORT had already gone to sleep – so we thought. But then he appeared in the door, standing there wide-legged like Django, looking from one to the other. Did he perhaps need to go outside again one more time tonight? We sensed that it was something else because he had this smirk on his face. *"What is it, SPORT?"* He turned around and walked away, looking back to see whether one of us was following him. I got up and he led me straight to his couch in the back room, jumping on it, curling up and reaching at me with one of his front paws. *"You little rascal, you have your way of communicating what you want, don't you,"* I smiled at him. It was very obvious, he wanted to snuggle and cuddle. He seemed to like this especially before going to sleep. So I gave him some hugging and stroking units that night, and he was happy. This became our ritual and he expected to be tucked in like this about every night, if not, he would appear again in the door, letting us know that something was missing. This dog had us trained more than we ever imagined.

SPORT was a real affectionate little guy. Sometimes during the day out of the blue his love was coming down. He would turn up with this look on his face, making it clear that smooching was on his mind. Although he normally seemed to consider the bed in our bedroom as a taboo zone for him, at those occasions he would jump up on it, snuggle into the blanket and sink his nose into the feather pillow. Peeking at us from the side, jerking all four of his stretched-out legs, he showed with a wide smile on his face how good he was feeling. Then he would reach out with his front paw, holding my arm down and conveying *"come on, I want some stroking units."* Of course I could not withstand, rolling him around, rubbing and petting him, scritching his belly until he tossed his hind legs. Had SPORT been a cat, I am sure that his purring would have made the air vibrate. But he was not a cat and he had his very own individual ways of expressing his happiness. He used to bend and cuddle his head into the bow of my arm and when I smooched him behind his ears – he always smelled so good – SPORT pressed his head against my face and we would be rubbing cheek to cheek. George, overlooking this and shaking his head, used to tease us, *"oh, how sweeeet!"* SPORT, lifting his head, peeked over to George, blinking his eyes as he always did when he was real content, *"come on and join us!"* So, there we were, having a threesome snuggling party.

Jiving

SPORT loved to listen to music. Besides Jazz, R&B and Soul, he had a special liking for the songs of James Brown or similar rather hard rhythms. If the music was turned on in the living room, SPORT immediately turned up in the door, looking excited, wagging his little stumpy tail, or he would just settle down right in front of the loudspeakers. This was amazing, as dogs have very keen and sensitive ears, but the noise did not seem to bother SPORT. He just lay there, his eyes following the actions of George or me how we were moving along with the beat, clapping our hands. *"Crazy homo sapiens,"* he must have been thinking. Sometimes, George took SPORT by his front legs, lifting him up a little bit, *"come on SPORT, shake your booty!"* And did he shake it! Standing upright on his hind legs, he would do a few steps along with George's leading hands. SPORT enjoyed this immensely, he just loved to be part of the pack and do what the others were doing too. When I clapped my hands to the beat of the music and moved them close to SPORT's face, he started to follow them around, first with his eyes, then also with his nose and head. Then his whole body began to move to the rhythm of the music, to and forth, and to the left and to the right. He was stepping forward and to the back and to the side and motioned his head up and down. He really seemed to be dancing, all the while following those swaying hands while they were slowly moving around in front of him. SPORT was great company to be with and he obviously enjoyed being included in our actions, strange as they may have appeared to him.

Airborne

SPORT was very curious. He had to stick his nose into everything that was going on around us. Which was okay, as it would let him learn and make him smarter? One day, though, this – combined with his temperament – cost him almost serious injury.

The person living in the apartment above us had accidentally dropped something off her balcony. It had fallen onto the roof right below our balcony and we were trying to shove it off down into the yard with a long broomstick. SPORT – at that time still quite young, not a year old yet – excitedly raced up and down alongside the railing of the balcony, barking and hampering us in what we were trying to do. *"Bark, bark, bark!"* So we ordered him to get out of the way and inside the house. Not realizing that SPORT was trying to find a different way to satisfy his curiosity, we kept on in our attempt to retrieve the dropped device.

And then I saw him! My heart almost stopped! I screamed! SPORT came flying off our kitchen balcony, which reached to the corner of the house, also overlooking the back balcony where we were scuffling around. Seconds later SPORT crash-landed on the concrete surface of the yard. I thought this was the end! He seemed to be slightly bouncing when he touched down, landing on all four feet, just like a cat. George, who was inside when he heard me cry out, thought that I had fallen off the balcony and came running outside while I raced inside past him, just screaming *"Sport jumped off the balcony, Sport jumped off the balcony!"*

We hastened to the door to get downstairs as fast as possible. But then we almost stumbled over SPORT, who was standing right in front of our apartment door! He had been able to get up by himself and run up the stairs. He was bewildered, looking at us with wide confused and frightened eyes, shaking strongly. He did not seem to really fathom yet what had happened.

While George was further checking SPORT for any possible injuries, I called the vet to make sure that he was there and to prepare him that we were going to come in an emergency. By now, George had already left with SPORT and I was hurrying to catch up with them. The vet's office was about three blocks away, but when I arrived, George and SPORT were not there yet. My goodness, where could they possibly be? Worried, I stepped outside again to see where they went.

Finally I saw them, George had been slowly walking SPORT part of the way to check on his overall behavior and to see whether his movements were normal or whether he might have blood in his urine. Nothing seemed to be abnormal.

The vet had everything prepared and immediately examined and x-rayed SPORT. No bones were broken, no internal injuries, and no internal bleedings. It was a miracle, after all, the jump off the balcony was at least about five meters or 17 feet above the ground. We were relieved! SPORT must have had a Guardian Angel! He was given some medication to make sure that no bleedings would occur at a later stage.

During the following days, SPORT walked around a bit stiff-legged, but there were no other symptoms indicating any problem. His appetite was normal and this event did not seem to slow him down at all.

Being back home again, we tried to analyze how this could have happened. SPORT always used to sit quietly on the benches along the sides of the kitchen balcony, just resting his snout on the railing and watching what was happening outside. He never bothered trying to jump over the railing, even when his imagined archenemy, the mailman, appeared. Then he would simply either bark or walk inside to the apartment door and let us know that there was somebody coming.

However, this time the back end of the kitchen balcony was blocked off, as I had placed two large flower pots on the bench to work on them later. In his eagerness to watch how we were struggling to get the dropped item off the roof below the other balcony, SPORT must have been racing toward the end of the balcony and – seeing the bench being blocked – just took a giant leap in order to jump over the flower pots to get in a position enabling him to watch the ongoing action this way.

But big surprise, there was no room to land on behind the flower pots! So he became airborne, totally unexpected and not retractable. He could not even get panicky because all of it happened so fast and was over in a few seconds. The fact that he did not fall but jump over the railing was to me the only explanation that he was lucky enough not to get injured more seriously. Had he fallen, he more than likely would have tumbled over and would have fallen on his head or side and really been harmed. But since he took a leap, his feet came first and his whole body was geared to land just like a cat on all four, which sort of cushioned the drop. And in addition, as he was not yet fully-grown and his bones must have still been somewhat on the flexible side, this bolstered it even further.

We were just happy that he was still in one piece. First we believed that SPORT as a result might have become fearful of heights, but this was not the case at all. He still wanted to sit out there on the balcony, look around and alarm us if someone strange dared to come too close to the door. He never tried to stand up at the railing or ever jump again. But I made sure that there was nothing blocking his access to his beloved watch-benches anymore.

The Big Helper

SPORT loved to be with his pack. If he could be with either George or me - who would count as his pack – his world was in order. He wanted to be part of everything we did and if he could do some chores, he was the happiest dog around.

Doing the Laundry

If I was standing at the ironing board, spraying the laundry to be ironed, he was either lying nearby or nudging me for some action. In this case, action meant using the fizz of the spraying bottle toward him. He loved to snap at the mist coming from the spray-nozzle. And – while squinting his eyes – he never minded his face getting wet. So the ironing chore went along like this, one fizz on the laundry, one fizz at SPORT, another fizz on the laundry and another one at SPORT. He really was a great help in getting the work done! But we were having fun!

Sewing Partner

The time that I was about to sew, was another chance for him to sign himself up for assistance. In order to have enough space to cut some material, I used to unfold a sewing board to be laid down on the floor in the middle of the room. This was like an invitation for SPORT to run up, jump on the board, sliding and rolling around. He then would lie down, all four stretched out and occupying the territory as his own, stretching his head down on his forefeet and mischievously watching his surroundings from under his long eyebrows.

At other times, SPORT just stood in the door, peeking around the corner, watching me. He waited until I had placed the textile on the board. And as soon as I had arranged the pattern and was getting ready to cut, he walked over to me with a wide smile on his face, his little stumpy tail working overtime. *"SPORT, don't you dare step on this material. Get away!"* His smile got wider and his eyes began to sparkle. And then he slammed himself right down in the middle of my sewing material. I tried to get him off there. It was no use, he stiffened all up, unwilling to leave, grinning all the way while I was sliding him across and off the cardboard. It was a fun game for him. While I was rearranging my sewing material, he sometimes came right back, reaching out with his front paw and smacking it at my arm, *"come on, I want to play",* or – dare you – he was planting a smooch on my cheek. How could I ever be mad with this charming little rascal, he had me all wrapped around his little toe. I would let him get away with murder. I loved him dearly!

The Gardener

One sunny afternoon I was working on our balcony, planting new flowers. SPORT was right with me, running around and watching my actions. Nudging my arm, sticking his nose into the dirt, looking at me real curious he seemed to ask, *"What are you doing there?"* *"I am planting some flowers for you to sniff at, SPORT. You love flowers, don't you?"* I held one of the new plants at his nose. With big eyes and wide nostrils he took in the scent, looking at me real seriously. *"Is it okay, SPORT?"* He did not object. So I kept on with my work.

In one corner, we had this very large flowerpot with a currant plant in it. Beneath the plant, the bottom was covered with weeds, which I carefully removed. After filling in some fresh dirt and smoothing it out evenly, I planted a few flowers separately and apart from each other below the currant plant, all under the watchful eyes of a very attentive SPORT. Finally I was finished with everything, glancing around and being content with the new look of our balcony. I had gone inside to wash up after this rather grubby work, when George called me *"come and see what your dog is doing!"* MY dog? This sounded serious. Well, what was MY dog doing? He was standing next to the big pot with the currant plant, holding one flower in his mouth, two lying next to him on the ground. *"No, SPORT, no! Don't do this!"* He had started to remove plant after plant from the pot, just as he had seen me do before with the weeds. Only he did not know the difference between weeds and flower plants. *"Oh, SPORT, what am I going to do with you?"* He looked at me with big innocent eyes as if to say, *"I was just trying to help you with your work."* *"Well, come on, big helper, we are going to put these flowers back into the soil again, where they can grow and become pretty."* He watched me repairing the damage, then made a move to rip one of the flowers out once more. *"No, SPORT, I said NO!"* He seemed to disagree with me. Did he perhaps think of these plants as not belonging there and being a foreign body on the smooth and even surface of the soil as I had prepared it after ripping out the weeds? SPORT was kind of orderly (believe it or not), also inside the house. When something was not at its place or something different showed up at a place where it did not belong, he would call our attention to it. Anyway, after another sharp *"NO"* he left the plants alone and never bothered them again. SPORT did not care anymore, he had dropped the idea of making a career as a gardener.

The Delivery Man

SPORT was always happy when he was allowed to do something useful. He was not as accurate, though, as a neighbor's beautiful Ridgeback, who proudly carried in his mouth a small basket with fresh rolls every morning from the bakery home to his owner. But if George or I had bought a paper, SPORT insisted to carry it for us. He would be jumping up at us, *"give it to me, give it to me"*. So we rolled the paper up to make it easier for him to hold it in his mouth. And proudly, holding his head high up, he would carry it along. If it was a rather thin paper, SPORT walked up the stairs to the apartment door, then drop it, looking at us for approval, wagging his stumpy tail. *"Good job, SPORT, well done"*, we would praise him, patting him on the head. And SPORT was proud as can be. But there were other times, when the paper seemed to be too thick and therefore heavy. Then SPORT simply dropped it somewhere on the way when he got tired of it and leave it for us to pick up.

SPORT knew exactly when the time was for me to come home from work. If I happened to be a little late, he would run over to George, look at him and say *"peep??"* *"Yes, I know, SPORT, she'll be here any minute."* And then his keen ears must have heard someone rattling at our mailbox downstairs. That used to be the sign for him. Running to George, *"there she is, there she is"*, then sprinting to the front door, excitedly waiting for George to open the apartment door so he could race downstairs to greet me. Everyone who has ever had a dog can understand how much joy this show of affection can give you. After the first stormy love attack was over, SPORT turned to business. He had a job to do, he wanted to carry the mail. *"Ok, SPORT, I let you carry this letter."* But no, he insisted on transporting the whole load. *"Ok, here you go."* Eager as he was, however, SPORT was a sloppy mailman. It was good that I walked up the stairs behind him, that way being able to pick up all the pieces he sometimes left as a trail behind.

SPORT was not only fond of carrying our paper or mail. During wintertime I had a problem convincing him that my gloves were for me to wear and not for him to parade around with. As soon as I put my leather gloves on I could see SPORT glancing at my hands, taking aim and jumping up, grabbing and pulling at my glove, then take off running. Of course he liked the chase when I tried to take the loot away from him. But meanwhile my hands were getting cold! I believe, just because these gloves were made from leather, they gave SPORT the impression that he was carrying some real animal prey. Sometimes, when George returned home from a walk with SPORT, this helpful and socially inclined dog walked into the house, proudly carrying one of George's leather gloves as well. So I was not alone in this game.

SPORT, the Gourmet

Dog Diet

While SPORT was still a puppy, he was first being fed four and then three times a day. Later on, after he was grown, two meals a day made him happy. It was fun watching him eat with such an enormous and healthy appetite. We had set fixed times when he could expect to get his food, we wanted him to have a regular schedule for eating and – matched to that – his walks outside. So he developed an inner clock. When we were just a few minutes late for his time to eat or to walk, he would come to us, checking what was going on. If we did not react immediately, he waited a while, left again and then came back, just giving us this intense look. He waited another short while and then kneaded the floor with his front feet and eventually bit the air in our direction. *"Snap!"* If this did not help, he would do a slight *"woof!"* Still being ignored, he put a little more force behind the *"woof!"* and then came closer, sometimes smacking us with one of his front paws, *"hey, what is it with you, I am hungry!"* This usually got our attention and we fixed his dish.

He loved his dried crispy dog food, freshly boiled rice and different kinds of meat. The meat normally included cooked beef, very seldom and only on special occasions also raw beef. But he would not reject canned dog food either. Then there were the chicken gizzards, chicken hearts and sometimes liver, he was crazy about liver. When these were boiling on the stove, SPORT would be sitting at the entrance to the kitchen, nose up in the air, and his eyes seemed to hypnotize the cooking pot in the hope to make the meat get ready sooner.

Of course, when George and I were eating at the table, he was eager to know what it was and perhaps get a sample of it. However, there was a strict rule in the house: *"No food from the table for the dog"*. All our guests respected this and SPORT – at least most of the times – never tried to beg.

Special Treats

Anyway, we began to cook our starchy foods – like potatoes or noodles – without salt, so we could put a small amount to the side for SPORT to snack on later. When we were finished at the table and ready to get the kitchen cleaned up, SPORT usually received his little extra. Had spaghetti been on the menu, I used to take out a few of the long cooked noodles and dangle them in front of SPORT's nose. He loved this, jumping up, grabbing them and munching his way through to the other end. This was repeated several times and SPORT had his fun with it.

It was not just only fun to SPORT, but pure lust to eat, when we treated him with a boiled potato with gravy. The potato would be mashed up and topped with some sauce. His taste buds began to work overtime, he was chomping himself into a frenzy, letting off all these smothered smacking sounds while working through his dish. Even after the dish was empty and cleaner than having been washed, he kept on licking it, pushing it all the while around the kitchen floor. Then he would look up, lick his chops, his eyes showing sheer delight of having had such a delicious goody. He was a gourmet all right!

If George was cooking spaghetti, he usually picked a few and let me test them if they were already done. While I sampled them, SPORT came running *"me too, me too"*. It became a ritual, when I tasted one half of the spaghetti, SPORT would get the other half. SPORT must have been an Italian in a previous life because he loved pasta.

Late in the evenings or in the middle of the night I sometimes sneaked into the kitchen to see what I could secretly snack on. Secretly? No way! As soon as I tried to put something into my mouth, there was this feeling of two eyes piercing my back. When I turned around, you guessed it, there was our dog standing in the kitchen door, giving me this look *"Ha, I caught you! Where is my share?"* Yes, SPORT saw to it that he was never left out!

The Food Taster

And then there was Thanksgiving Day. I was in the kitchen preparing the stuffing for the turkey. Neck, giblet, heart and liver were already cooked. I was in the process of cutting them up to put them into the stuffing, while SPORT, nose up in the air, sniffing and taking in the scent of these goodies, had taken his strategic position, patiently waiting, watching every move I made. Sometimes in between he lifted his head, all of the ingredients smelled so good to him, the aroma was tickling his nose! He knew that he was going to get his fair share, after all, it was Thanksgiving Day! On a special occasion like this, SPORT had the important job of being a food taster, and naturally he took his job very seriously. I used to cut a slice of giblet and let him sample it. He looked at me approvingly. *"That's okay? You want one more?"* What a question! Of course he got another piece of giblet, then the rest was cut up for the stuffing, same procedure for neck, heart and liver. Especially the liver got his fancy, he was crazy about it. So this called for an extra portion, because he was such a good food taster. After everything was chopped and put into the stuffing, SPORT was satisfied and walked back into the other room to curl up in his nest, taking a nap.

Munching Party

In the evenings, when George and I were playing cards, reading or watching TV and having a bag of popcorn along with it, SPORT became part of this munching orgy. SPORT loved popcorn. He heard the corn popping on the stove and there he was, standing in the door with big hungry eyes. He expected to have his share, after all he was part of the pack. So it went like this: one big popped-out kernel for SPORT, who would chew it loudly with an open mouth, his eyes flashing in delight, then some big popped-out kernels for George, the next one again for SPORT and some more for George. This went on for a while and when George finally said *"that's enough"*, SPORT would walk over to my side and the game started all over again. The three of us were munching in unison, perfectly content.

Weird Tastes

SPORT also loved sweets. But we would never give him chocolate or similar candy, these actually can be very dangerous for the system of a canine! Carrots were the alternative. When I was preparing carrots for our own meals, I always gave SPORT a few thinly cut slices of this raw vegetable. He would take them on his tongue, relishing on the juice, then pull them into his mouth and – while looking at me real contentedly, blinking his eyes – chew on them, smacking loudly.

SPORT was always curious about anything we snacked on. So we often let him sniff at whatever it was, with the result that he wanted to taste it too. That way he began to like also raisins and nuts or cheese. As soon as he heard us crack a nutshell he would show up for his part of the goodies. However, he would not just eat anything that we let him sniff. Many of our human type of snacks did not turn him on, but at least he was satisfied that he was not missing anything that he otherwise might have wanted. And there was one thing he deeply disliked. If we had a glass of wine or any other drink of alcohol, and we went through the ritual of letting him get a whiff of it, he would wrinkle his nose, withdraw in disgust and give us a look of disapproval. Good so, SPORT, you were smarter than many humans.

Eerie! Eerie!

Moon Talk

"Ohaoooahooooooh! Ahooooahoooooooha!" George and I shot straight up in the bed in the middle of the night! Good grief, what was that? *"Ooahooooahooooooh!!"* There it was again! Half asleep, we got up to find out what was going on, following the howl we heard. And there he was, sitting on the balcony bench, snout way up in the air and howling at the moon *"ahoooahoooahoooooh!"* From afar somewhere in the city, there came the echo. Some other dog was sending a message too. Before SPORT would get the whole dog community stirred up and start a concert, we ordered him back in. *"Sport, you are going to get us evicted from this home. You got to cut this out!"* Reluctantly, SPORT came in, swallowing his last howl, his throat still throbbing. We never thought that his wolf ancestry would come through like this. At first the sound of it gave us goose pimples, but then we were sort of proud that he still had it in him. Anyway, we could not allow him to live this out in the city, there would have been too much adversity.

Infatuated

Being a dog and "having it in him", SPORT of course would do it again. But having this happen around three or four o'clock early in the mornings made it somewhat troublesome. First we did not grasp it why he always started his howl at this very same and absolutely ungodly time. But when we investigated we noticed that it always happened when the paperboy passed by, having his two dogs in tow. *"Aoooohaoooooooooh!"* Had SPORT become infatuated with one of the female dogs that the paperboy took along with him on his route, and did he want to get her attention this way? We didn't know, but *"aoohaohaoooooo-haooooh!"* it was hard to have SPORT stop doing this, it was part of his nature. At the first sounds, when he was pumping up for the howl, we were right beside him, telling him to cool it. This cost us a lot of sleep, and perhaps also the neighbors', but none of them ever complained.

The Magician

It was as if SPORT could do magic with his howl, though, especially to his fellow canines. One of our neighbors used to have the dog of an acquaintance over for dog-sitting now and then and usually placed him in his backyard. But this dog soon felt abandoned and lonely and he started to whine, whimper and cry. To hear this was kind of heartbreaking. SPORT must have felt the same way, because as soon as he heard the whimpering, he would rush to the balcony and jump on the bench, nose high in the air, working himself up to a howl, *"aoohaooohahooooooooooaoooh!"* Immediately the other dog stopped his crying, looking over at SPORT with big astonished eyes. For a while, both dogs were staring at each other from the distance. The neighbor's dog soon calmed down and SPORT ended his howl. It was amazing to see the other dog's reaction to SPORT's interference. It always worked, whenever this other dog came to visit the neighbor, being lonely and then whine, SPORT showed him that he was not alone and his howl soothed him down. *"Well, Dr. psych. SPORT, when are you going to open up your official practice?"*

Jungles of Madagascar

There were other situations when SPORT tried his "therapy". An animal film was shown on TV about a group of Lemurs noising up the jungles of Madagascar, when SPORT came running into the room, looking around bewildered and checking out what all these strange sounds were about. Were these creatures in some kind of trouble? It never failed, SPORT would lift his head and nose, draw up some air, his chest widening, and then a long and wailing *"ahoooahaooooooh!"*

was released. It was strange, if any dogs appeared on the screen and did some barking and yapping, SPORT never acted like this. But these Lemurs really stirred him up with their singing and chanting. He became absolutely excited: *"aoohaooo-haahooooooh!"* But what was going on, why didn't these guys show any respect of his howl? They just kept on doing their thing. SPORT seemed to be somewhat disappointed, as he did not understand that this was just TV and not reality. He was sitting there staring at the screen, looking at us and preparing again for another howl. Was he perhaps thinking that he could soothe them down as he did the neighbor's visiting dog? We don't know, but SPORT's magic definitely was not working here. And he had a hard time understanding this.

Roots

But there was another situation when SPORT could prove that his skills were working. After he was about a year old, we took him back to his roots – to the breeder – to show him proudly what had become of the puppy he once sold to us.

While we walked across the yard of the breeder's compound, all hell broke loose. There were several dens being home to the dogs of the breeder. And these dogs began to jump at the fences, barking and snarling and acting real aggressively.

It was a hairy situation. We doubted that SPORT recognized his mama, it was too long ago that he had seen her. He placed himself right between George and me, just sitting there for a while and looking at the ranting and raving dogs in the dens. Then he did it. He lifted his head way up to the back, snout in the air, and started a long and wailing howl, *"aoohaooohaoooooohoooooooh!"* It took us by surprise and the sound made us shiver! And it had an effect that we did not expect at all, it shut up all the dogs in the yard! Unbelievable! The other dogs stood there in their cages, staring at SPORT, and SPORT staring at them. It was suddenly real quiet! It was eerie! We never understood why other dogs would react to SPORT this way. We began to believe that SPORT had magic powers.

Into this silence there came the breeder walking out of his house to see who had come to visit him. He was a friendly, elderly man, just shaking his head about the dogs' actions. They kept quiet now and we were able to talk to the breeder. At first he teased us that SPORT would be so skinny, we should take a look at SPORT's brother who just raced toward us, jumping a fence and beginning to chase a very startled SPORT. SPORT's brother was the only one of the litter that the breeder had kept for himself. He was a strong and sturdy dog who really looked substantially bigger than our dog. But then the breeder laughed and told us that he had been feeding his dog some special food as a test and that he actually was a bit too hefty at the moment. He admired the way SPORT had developed, his body and posture. He was happy for us that SPORT had turned out to be a healthy, good-natured and lovable companion. Meanwhile, SPORT and his brother had become acquainted and they seemed to like each other. As a matter of fact, the brother ran and came back with a buffalo-skin bone and dropped it at SPORT's feet, and was now standing there in front of our dog, wagging his stumpy tail. This was most unusual, but the breeder laughed again, *"Well, this is the way he is, always bringing something to a person he likes."*

His Health

Visits to the Vet

SPORT was a strong and healthy little guy. Aside from his regular annual inoculations, he very seldom had to see the vet. And if he had to, he was not the least bit afraid of him as many other dogs are. As a matter of fact, when we passed by the outside of the vet's office, SPORT always wanted to pay him a visit and ran up the small stairs in front of it, waiting at the door to be let in. This evidently was caused by the VIP-treatment he usually got there. Whenever he saw the doctor and was given his annual shots, he would be awarded with a dog biscuit for holding still and being brave. Yet SPORT was a little trickster, after the vet had given him something, he went straight to the vet's helper and charmed her too into letting him have another goody.

But it was not always so pleasant for him to see the vet. There was this incident when SPORT had been frolicking around with a Pitbull. Both of them were not fully-grown yet and their play looked innocent enough. But then, all of a sudden, the other dog jumped at SPORT and bit him in the chest. There was some wrestling and screaming. George and the other owner grabbed the dogs apart and examined SPORT if he had any injuries. There was no blood, so it seemed that he got away unharmed. However, a few days later, SPORT developed a fever, he became weak and listless. His chest was swollen and sensitive. An X-ray at the vet's showed that SPORT had a slight abrasion on his chest bone, where a big fluid-filled blister had developed and was now inflamed. A dose of antibiotics took care of the infection, but SPORT had to come for several days in a row to have the swelling drained. This was an unpleasant and painful procedure and poor little SPORT was suffering quite a bit. We tried to comfort him as much as possible during the treatment while he was standing there, feeling uneasy but looking at us with big and trusting eyes, confident that we were doing the right thing for him, however uncomfortable it might be. He was okay again after a while, but we made sure that he never came in contact again with a Pitbull.

Every now and then, SPORT happened to step onto one of those grass ears with its bristly fibers during late summer, when the grass became dry and the grainy heads fell off. If these kept clinging to the hair between his pads and went unnoticed, this could mean trouble. Because they had the tendency to bore themselves right through the skin into the pads of his feet, where they would cause inflammation and of course pain with every step. The first time this happened, George and I thought that we could remove this pestering thing, but SPORT would scream murder and slaughter. And after a few tries we gave up as we realized, this thing could be pulled out only against its grain and that this would most likely cause more injury. So we took poor SPORT to the vet, where we had to hold the struggling patient down with three persons, while the doctor examined his foot. The end was that the vet put some poultice on his pads and wrapped his foot up real good and secured it with some water-resistant tape. SPORT was now sporting a big and heavy clubfoot. He sniffed at it, being disgusted and hobbled out of the vet's office on just three legs, holding his wrapped front foot way up ahead of him, giving everyone who cared to show him some sympathy an accusing look, *"you see, what they have done to me!"* But as offended as SPORT was at first, he adjusted quickly to his temporary handicap and managed to race around like always, it only sounded somewhat different: tip tip tip bonk…. tip tip tip bonk…. And after about one week, when the vet unwrapped the tape, the fibered grass spike had wandered through the foot, lying on top of his toes and could easily be removed. So SPORT had survived this ordeal and was his old spindle-legged self again.

Difficult Times

People used to tell us that SPORT was our child. In a way this was true. We loved and cared for him, as we would have for a child. We tried to show and teach him as much as possible and protect him whenever it seemed necessary. But there is one big difference, a child will eventually grow up and become independent, while your dog will always remain absolutely dependent on you. And this fact made SPORT become especially close to us. When we saw this total innocence in his eyes, this amiable naiveté, his trust in us and his never-ending loyalty, we also realized his vulnerability and we knew that we would never desert him, that we would want to be there for him at all times.

And there came the time when he really needed us. The situation sneaked up on us.

First Signs

It began one day when we were wrestling for a piece of cloth, one of SPORT's favorite games. *"It's mine!" "No, it's mine!" "Give it to me!" "No, you can't have it!" "Grrrrrr!" "Oh, come on!"* So it went on, to and forth, to and forth. Then suddenly one day SPORT screamed out, he backed away, looking at me with wide eyes, being terrified! *"What is it, little fellow?"* I was shocked. Had I hurt him? How? I had not been extra rough with him, just playing as always. Perhaps he had a bad tooth, having the condition aggravated by pulling on the cloth? I did not know. My first reaction was to take him in my arms to comfort him, trying to figure out what might have caused him to cry out in pain. But a short time later SPORT had forgotten all about it and settled down, taking a nap.

For a while, everything was normal with SPORT, he was the same as always. Then a similar thing happened again. We began to watch him more closely, considered taking him to the vet if it got worse. Then he started to develop problems when he routinely tried to stretch after getting up following a nap, or bending his head down when eating from his dish. In these cases where he stretched his head forward, SPORT involuntarily yelped in pain.

This was the time that we decided to have the vet look into this. The devastating news was that SPORT supposedly had a pinched nerve in his neck, perhaps caused by a slipped disk, which could paralyze all four of his legs if aggravated any further. If SPORT's condition would not get better from any conventional treatment, he would need an operation, where even the preliminary method to locate the exact site could be deadly.

The final details of an operation sounded so gruesome to us that we first wanted to get a second opinion from a nearby University vet clinic. For the time being, SPORT received a series of injections against any pain as well as some antibiotics, which he took quite well. He roamed around as if he had never had any problems.

Did he suffer a Stroke?

But this was deceiving. Because of his seemingly improved condition, we began to doubt the seriousness of his illness, but were soon shaken back into reality. SPORT had been lying in his hut sleeping, when he suddenly started to scream in terror. We rushed over to him and saw him struggling, trying to get up in vain. We helped him to get out of his hut. SPORT's body was rigid and cramped up in a zigzag, his right side seemed paralyzed. He was not able to stand on his right-side feet. SPORT's screams were heartbreaking. We were sure that he was having a stroke. But just as suddenly as this came up, it stopped the same. While George was holding SPORT, I called the vet that we were coming right away. He gave SPORT some fast-acting, strong pain-reducing and anti-inflammatory injections, followed by a temporary soft laser therapy. At the same time he explained to us that dogs could not have a stroke, which we did not believe because of the typical signs that SPORT showed during the following time.

Although SPORT seemed to be as lively as ever again following this initial treatment, we noticed that he held his head slightly toward the right, he also shook his head quite often and scratched his right ear. Also, he could not make his right ear stand up anymore. It hung down weakly while the other ear on the left side could be lifted and twisted normally. This gave SPORT a mischievous look, but we knew better. In addition, there were more signs that he had suffered a stroke. His right eye was constantly running in contrast to his left eye. And his mouth was slightly shifted to the right, which could not be detected though by an unsuspecting onlooker, as SPORT's beard was covering this condition. SPORT's beard also covered – and went unnoticed by us for some time – that saliva was constantly running from the right corner of his mouth, which made it difficult to keep his beard untangled and keep it from matting, so that we had to brush and comb it constantly. It seemed that the whole right side of SPORT's body was affected by this incident.

The Vet Clinic

Our next step was to make an appointment at the University's vet clinic. They examined

SPORT quite differently from the way that our local vet did. They also did not think that he had a stroke. However, to find out what had caused the problems, they wanted us to bring SPORT back the following week to keep him there for a while to run tests and have him treated properly. We were eager to learn what was troubling our loyal friend, hoping that – whatever caused his condition – it could be cured and SPORT would be his old spry self again.

So it was decided, SPORT would be going into the hospital. Next Monday morning we loaded him into the car and off we went. We were not allowed to let SPORT keep anything during his stay that smelled like us, like an old shirt or towel, for him to perhaps not feel so deserted. We began to wonder how he would take it to be without either George or myself in a strange surrounding for a lengthy period. He had never been separated from us. This surely would make it harder for him this time. But the vets reassured us that dogs normally adjust quite easily, as they are also in contact with other animals around them. It would usually be the owner suffering more. Well, anyhow, we were kind of uneasy. SPORT was innocently fooling around on the back seat of the car, having no idea what was coming. After we arrived, he kept close by, curiously looking around. When all the paperwork was done, it was time to go. SPORT sensed that something different was in the air. He stood up on his hind legs, leaning his front paws on George, looking up at him with begging eyes, *"come on, let's go back home"*. *"SPORT, you are going to stay here for a while"*, we tried to explain to him, knowing that he would not understand. We petted his head and the vet's assistant put a house collar and leash on SPORT and led him away. SPORT easily went along, but kept turning around to see what was going on, why we stayed behind and were not coming with him. He was taken way down the long hallway and he obviously was confused. So were we. We quickly walked out the other way, getting out of SPORT's sight, very heavy-hearted. Almost all the way home, we hardly spoke a word. We felt as if we had deserted him. Was he going to be all right?

While we were not allowed to visit SPORT to spare him the agony of parting and leaving him behind over and over again, a call every second day was desirable and expected so we could be informed about his progress. I could hardly wait to call in and hear how SPORT was doing. I was told that he had adjusted well and also took the food they offered him, which was a good sign. So far they found that he had an inflammation of the middle ear and they strongly suspected meningitis as well. But as he was being treated right away intravenously with heavy doses of antibiotics, this could never be clarified completely. The vets settled for the diagnosis vestibular-syndrome. It was clear, though, that the swellings caused by the ear infection had pressured on brain and nerves, causing the pain and breakdown of his system. Any swelling in the head close to the brain is a potentially dangerous condition. However, the treatment with antibiotics, cortisone and vitamin Bs was taken well by SPORT and he was on his way to recovery.

Back with his Pack again

Then the longest and loneliest two weeks were over and we could finally pick up SPORT to bring him home again. We were looking forward to see him race toward us and greet us happily. But what a disappointment! When SPORT was brought into the waiting room, he seemed to be in a stupor. With a blank look in his eyes he walked toward us, sniffing and, yes, recognizing us, but hardly showing any emotions. All he wanted was to get away from here, get outside and do some of his business, as if he had been held back from doing that too long. While George walked him around outside on a patch of grass, I finished the paper work and then we finally were on our way back home. SPORT was glad to see us, but he appeared to be totally confused. He did not seem to trust the situation yet, that he was back with his pack again and back to his normal surroundings. His coat was dull and dirty and smelly. His belly and part of his head and neck were naked, shaven in order to make the examinations and treatments easier. And his hind legs were swollen and inflamed from the infusions they had given him. We assumed that in a teaching hospital – that's how I see a University hospital – not everyone is an experienced M.D. yet, but rather still some of the students have to get their training on the living object. It must have been a real trauma for SPORT, being in a strange surrounding without anyone of his pack, having all those strange people fumble on his body, sticking all those needles into him and probably hurting him. How could he understand that this was necessary in order to learn what caused his problems and to find the appropriate treatment? We felt really sorry and guilty that we had SPORT exposed to that, but then again, they found what was wrong with our dog and helped him to get better again. For that we were thankful.

First thing that SPORT did before following us to our apartment, was to race up the three steps to Markus' barber shop, placing himself in the middle of the open door, lying down and watching his surroundings outside, inhaling this familiar sight. We let him be. He needed to readjust again, orientate himself where he was and believe that his nightmare had ended. After a little while, he followed us upstairs to our place, where he ran through every room, inspecting every corner, sniffing his way around. Yes, he was back home again! With his pack! And everything was as it was before he was taken to the clinic! He went into the kitchen to look for his water dish, and then he slurped and slurped and slurped. He was really thirsty!

After a short rest, he let George take him into the bathtub and give him a thorough soaping up. SPORT for the first time in his life seemed to enjoy this one. It washed off all the smell and the pain, the fear and the loneliness from the time at the hospital and made him come closer to being the real SPORT again. However, it still took SPORT about another week or so to finally adjust completely and to understand that he was really, really back home with his pack again.

Continuing Problems

As happy as we were that SPORT was with us again, some problems still persisted during the following time. The vet clinic had given us a stack of medication that SPORT was supposed to keep taking for a while. The antibiotics and vitamins B were well tolerated by him, but the cortisone was affecting him severely. He could not control his bladder any more. When he kept having accidents in the house he became very embarrassed and confused, he did not understand what was happening to him. Of course we did not scold SPORT for the mess, it was not his fault, he was still sick.

One afternoon when I came back into the house from running some errands, SPORT nudged me, trying to get my attention and then led me to the balcony, where he stopped in front of a large puddle. He looked up at me, then again at the pool, his face and whole body being the living bad conscience. He appeared so guilty, his head down, peeking at me from the side. *"Hey, little man, I know you didn't mean to do this"*, I comforted him while wiping the ground. *"This medication is giving you hell, isn't it?"* I was glad that I had taken off from work for the next two weeks, so George and I could take turns in taking SPORT downstairs every two hours or so. The cortisone could not be stopped abruptly, but it was to be gradually reduced. And SPORT still had to endure the effects for some time, however slowing down until he was back to normal after about a couple of weeks.

New Vet

Meanwhile, we had found another vet to continue SPORT's treatment. SPORT was still very sensitive about his ears, which needed to be taken care of. His defenses seemed to be quite down because by now he had also caught a painful throat infection, which made him cough and his voice sounded very coarse. The vet advised us to wrap something warm around SPORT's throat to back up the other medication he prescribed. So I cut one of my old woolen shawls in half and with the help of a piece of Velcro made it fit right for his neck. Now he looked like Mr. Cool with this reddish-brown wrap on his neck! SPORT did not mind and we took the remarks of passers-by with humor when they asked if this was the newest fashion for dogs.

However, things got worse when SPORT in addition developed some kind of problem with his front feet. His pads began to swell slowly and made it difficult for him to walk. The vet was not of much help here, as the treatment he suggested did not help at all. And to top the situation off, SPORT became more and more agitated with the vet, he did not like him. It developed to the point where SPORT began to growl at the vet whenever he put his hands on him. This could not go on, so we looked once again for another animal doctor. Talking to other dog owners, you get a lot of feedback about the different vets of the neighborhood.

So we found this new doctor. But the change turned out to be absolutely worse after a few visits. This guy had two Ridgebacks, beautiful dogs. But this one day when we walked into the practice, the male Ridge was not restricted to his usual area and unexpectedly appeared in the waiting room, no doctor or assistant nearby. He first showed no signs of aggression against SPORT, but nevertheless – it happened so fast – all of a sudden and out of the blue this large dog reached out and grabbed SPORT in the middle and began shaking him wildly. George and I jumped on him, trying to make the Ridge let go of SPORT. The situation was horrible, we feared for SPORT's life. Then the Ridge gave up and SPORT was free again, but he definitely was injured although there was no outside bleeding. Meanwhile the vet had come in and – pale-faced – quickly put SPORT under the X-ray to see the extent of the injuries.

SPORT had suffered some internal bleeding and a large hematoma was developing at his belly. The vet gave him some injections to stop any further bleeding and to soothe the pain, but SPORT walked around very stiff-legged and obviously in misery during the following days. We were to rub his swollen belly with some salve the vet had given us and to wrap it with an elastic bandage. Poor SPORT, we had taken him to the vet for help, and instead he came out being in worse shape than before. We were absolutely angry with the vet and let him know this. But the damage was done and the doctor tried his best to get SPORT back on his feet. It took quite a while with a series of injections and pills and salve and bandaging and a lot of tender loving care from George and me until SPORT became healthy again.

But it was only a short period of relative well-being. A few weeks later on a Sunday morning, SPORT began to throw up violently and kept going like this on and on. This seemed not to be one of the temporary nausea that dogs sometimes show for no apparent reason. We became alarmed and – in absence of a different vet that would know SPORT already and be on call on a weekend – called up our previous vet who told us to bring SPORT in immediately because this might be poisoning. We were not aware that SPORT had perhaps picked up something from the street and ate it, as he knew that he was strictly forbidden to do so. But one could never be totally sure.

When we arrived at the doctors' he gave SPORT some injections. Then he insisted to keep our dog over night to run some tests. That was when we objected, we did not really trust this guy enough anymore with our dog without us being present. He became displeased and harshly said *"Well, then you do this yourselves"*, handing us some barium that we were to inject into SPORT's mouth to swallow and then come back in the morning in order for him to X-ray SPORT to find out if he had any problems in his digestive tract. It was all done this way and we were absolutely glad that we did not leave SPORT behind at his clinic for reasons we learned much later. SPORT had stopped vomiting and his system seemed to calm down by now. The next morning we went for the scheduled X-ray and the doctor did not find anything disturbing. But he gave our dog a further series of three injections. On our repeated inquiries what they contained, he only mumbled something unintelligible. No, this was not a vet that would get everybody's confidence. He made us uneasy. We regretted coming here once more and vowed it to be the last time.

Not long after arriving home again with SPORT, he seemed to become listless and weak. He lied down and rested. He did not want to get up any more. We did not understand, as for a while he seemed to be getting better. He had not been drinking anything all day. When we came checking on him, he just looked sadly up at us, his nose and eyes glowing with fever. Was it something the vet had injected into him? Hard to believe, but meanwhile we had heard stories about this particular doctor and our distrust was growing. We brought SPORT some water to drink. He refused. We brought him some of his favorite food. He refused. We tried to make his fever go down in putting a cool damp cloth intermittently on his nose or the pads of his feet. He just looked at us with big and sad eyes, whimpering occasionally. *"SPORT, what is happening to you"*, we were getting desperate. He was developing into such a poor state that we began to believe that he would not survive the next few days. Tender loving care and attention alone was not enough, he also needed to get some liquid or light food in him or he would become too dehydrated. We kept trying to entice him to take a slurp of water, and if it would be just a little bit. We came to his bed and held the dish in front of him, and then finally he dragged his tongue through the water once. It was not much, but it helped. Any little bit he took in would help. We went through several kinds of food, he rejected all of it. Then we brought him some cottage cheese. He had never eaten it before, but now he took several tiny bits. The try was worth it, it seemed to be good to him. And the fact alone that he accepted this small amount gave us some hope. We let him have a little rest and then tried again. We gave him all the affection we could while hand-feeding him piece by piece tiny amounts of cottage cheese, being happy that he at last began to take in some kind of food and liquid, however little it was. Yes, SPORT made it through the night and slowly recovered during the following days, while gratefully accepting our special care and love.

When other dog owners heard about what happened to SPORT, quite a few similar stories turned up, all involving this same vet giving their pets this series of three injections, which seemed to make several of them even sicker. One cat had died while staying at his clinic and the vet refused to turn her body over to the owner. So rumors popped up that he might do experiments on animals. I didn't know what was true about all of this, I only was glad that we had not left SPORT under this doctor's "care" over night when he asked us to. Months later, we learned that this particular vet had to close his practice. The reasons why were hushed up, but everyone in the neighborhood had their own speculations about this. And those need not to be discussed any further.

It became clear that it was not easy to find the right veterinarian for your pet. The first one we had for SPORT was all right for several years, as he needed to give him only his regular yearly inoculations or perhaps treat an injury on his foot. But then he did not detect the seriousness of SPORT's ear infection and possible meningitis and that he had a stroke, and instead wanted to operate a supposed pinched nerve in his neck, which – we are sure today – SPORT would not have survived in his condition at that time. The next animal doctor seemed to have no sense for animals, he was harsh and rough and impatient and SPORT did not tolerate him. The next one had our dog leaving his practice sicker than he was when coming in, twice. So we were desperate to find the right vet because SPORT needed continuous treatment, as his condition was still quite poor.

Other pet owners told us about a woman veterinarian who had done a great job with their pets. She was somewhat controversial, though, as she came across as quite resolute and very direct, which scared some sensitive people away. Well, we definitely preferred a straightforward person, and all we wanted was someone to take SPORT's ailments serious and help him. So we tried her out.

The first time we went to her, she lived up to her reputation, as she scolded us for not having brought in our dog earlier. But then she listened to his story and examined him thoroughly and found several things that urgently needed attention right away, while other problems could be taken care of when his condition had already improved somewhat. She explained everything to us in detail and made a plan on how to follow through, one step at a time.

First things to be tackled were the local symptoms of SPORT's feet, ears and private parts. The vet explained that he had a typical triple infection, as dogs usually lick their feet and their body and then, while scratching their ears with their feet, could be passing on any existing infection to these areas. So, as none of the previous treatments seemed to have helped much, we were to give SPORT eardrops and he was to take antibiotics internally and in addition needed regular foot baths several times a week with a disinfecting solution, followed by a treatment with a soothing salve.

Now, making SPORT accept all of this was a real challenge. Giving him the eardrops and pills was relatively easy compared to the foot baths, which he deeply resented – at first. I made him stand in the big bath tub with his front feet soaking in a smaller dish containing the lukewarm disinfecting solution. SPORT stood there, looking at me, his eyes begging from under his long eyebrows. He was "pumping up" and it sounded like he was sobbing *"peep, peep, I don't like this"*. If I did not watch, he would simply take his feet out of the dish and stand beside it. I tried to take his attention away from the disliked procedure of soaking his feet in telling him stories, talking to him, while keeping him company and petting him.

But then later, after having rinsed and dried his feet, the real struggle began. SPORT, always having been prissy about his feet, acted very peculiar when I was to put the salve on them. At first he let me lift one of his front feet, acting as if he was going to hold still, but pulled away at the very last moment, his eyes telling me *"ha, I tricked you!"*

It became a matter of who was going to trick whom. If I succeeded in rubbing the salve on his feet, I still had to stop him from licking it off immediately. So I quickly slipped a baby sock on each of his front feet and fastened it with a little tape. Now it was SPORT's turn again. *"I show you what I think of this"*, and he blitzed through the house, settled down on "his" couch in the back and frantically ripped and gnawed at the socks until only a few strings and threads and a ring of the tape still stuck on his legs.

The following time we went through many nerve-tearing and who-is-going-to win sessions like this, until the medication seemed to take effect. SPORT began to understand that this procedure, however disliked by him, was beneficial to his condition and he finally held still whenever I treated his feet.

Of course it was also helpful that he was being rewarded with a goody afterwards, as we knew that this time was a very hard one for SPORT. As a matter of fact, when the state of his feet had improved and the intervals between his treatments became longer, he sometimes even waited by the bathroom door, wondering why he was not getting his usual "therapy".

New Baby in the House?

This was also the time where neighbors began to wonder what was going on in our house. Lately there were rows and rows of baby socks drying on the clothing line. Did they have a new baby over there? No, all these tiny socks belonged to

SPORT. I had bought a whole bunch of socks, as SPORT was to wear them only once, then they needed to be washed and disinfected before being used again so that they would not re-infect SPORT's precious feet. SPORT had to wear them

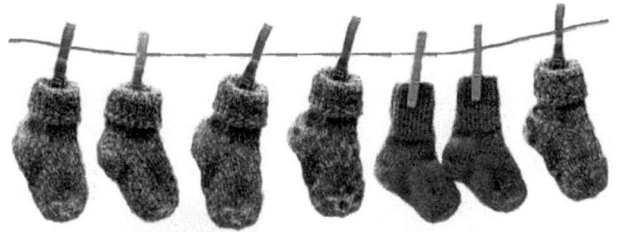

also outside on his walks, which made us have to listen to all kinds of remarks from passers-*by "oh, look at the new bootee style" or "where are the other two, did they get lost in the washing machine?"* We took those remarks with a smile, as the socks did serve their purpose in our case.

Walking Dispensary

It took several months until the condition of SPORT's feet had normalized. And this was only possible through absolutely consequent treatment with a lot of medication and remedies which needed to be switched every so often in order for them not to lose effectiveness.

Every now and then we tried to stop the antibiotics to see if SPORT could live without them. But every time, after two weeks or so, the bad symptoms came back again, which meant that SPORT had to continue taking these drugs forever. Here, he also tried to trick us many times in making us believe that he had swallowed the pill. We noticed that he was eating around the pill if we had mixed it in his regular food, leaving it lying lonely in his empty dish. We began to wrap it in a piece of meat or canned food, hand-feeding it to him. But he was no fool and mostly detected if a piece was spiked, and we later found the pill lying somewhere in a corner. And soon SPORT became distrustful even when we gave him a special treat, sniffing at everything suspiciously. We did not want to use force in giving SPORT his medicine, so we tried out several ways.

And finally, we overcame the problem, just playing on his greediness. The pill was put into a boiled chicken heart, one of his greatest favorites and a perfect cover for the pill as it had this little hole in the middle into which the pill could be slid easily. He was first fed a regular chicken heart, which – after sniffing at it carefully – he greedily grabbed from the hand, followed by the spiked one, which was immediately chased with another normal heart. This way he had no choice but to swallow the pill and didn't even realize it. *"Ha, SPORT, this time we tricked you!"*

It got to the point, where we had to make a chart, at what times SPORT was to take which medication and what dose of it, as he was not only treated for his feet and ears, but he had also developed a heart condition as well as prostrate problems and needed special medication for all of it. So we carefully spaced the different drugs like antibiotics, heart medication, vitamin pills, painkillers, antiseptics and soothing salves during the day, morning, noon and evening, coordinated with his meals and walks outside.

However, beside the fact that SPORT had become a walking dispensary, there was an unexpected positive side effect of all this medication. No fleas or ticks ever came near our dog anymore, the medication must have worked like a repellent. With time, his condition had improved tremendously and we were very satisfied with the new veterinarian. SPORT seemed to like her as well and he never hesitated when we went to see her for routine check-ups.

SPORT, the Senior

When SPORT's health problems began, he was about eight years old. Now, having most of the obvious ailments overcome, he was nearly eleven. And once again, he was lively, frisky, curious and eager to go on top of the world. That's why I was surprised when our vet one day referred to SPORT as being a senior now. What? SPORT a senior? No way! I could still only see the spunky, funny, mischievous and always being-up-to-something companion in him. He had not slowed down a bit. But then again, if one day he would be slowing down, he surely would be in the most understanding and caring hands. George and I would take good care of him. The vet had just made us aware of the fact, that dogs don't stay young forever either.

Well, as for the time being, SPORT seemed to be far away from being old. He loved again to take us on long walks. He had not forgotten where the rabbits played their pranks and still wanted to chase them. He also had not forgotten the pampering he received while being ill and now he was not willing to give up any of his so hard-earned privileges. Quite to the contrary, he tried to extend them. During the time of his weak health, we had done everything possible to make it a bit easier for him, we had pampered and spoiled him and told ourselves *"so what, is it so bad that he gets this little extra attention?"* We wanted him to be happy and understand that we were there for him, no matter what. If he had become spoiled, then we were the ones who had to deal with that. It did not bother us, it only amused us to watch him how he was trying to keep his benefits.

Before, while it was sometimes strenuous for him to go for a walk, we had given him an extra goodie after coming home, just for him having been so brave. Fine, but now he insisted on it. If we overlooked this, he walked straight into the kitchen and sat in front of the corner where he knew that we kept his treats on a rack at the wall. Staring up at them, giving us a short glance from the side and then again pointing his nose at the desired goodies, it looked as if he was trying to hypnotize them to jump voluntarily into his mouth. This – unfailingly – made us melt. So he usually received his "leckerli" from the one who had just walked him.

But after a while, this seemed not enough. If George had walked him and had given him his treat, SPORT walked straight over to me and claimed another one. It was the same the other way around. Unaware of his newest trickery, George or I promptly fell for this and gave him the desired goodie, assuming the other forgot to do that.

But soon we looked through this little rascal's charming scam and how he mastered to play fiddle with us. So SPORT had to change his mode of operandi. Now he tried to make up for the refused double dipping after an occasional walk in putting up a show after every walk, no matter how often a day we went outside with him. But there was only so much that we could let him get away with, we had to watch his diet too. More than once friends asked us if SPORT wasn't getting somewhat on the hefty side. Hefty? What were they talking about? Not our SPORT! It only seemed this way because he had a thick fur at that time…!? Yeah, yeah, I know! Okay, we finally came around to realize that we only lied to ourselves. So we decided that it was better to cut down on the extra treats for SPORT and he would have only an occasional goody, accompanied with ample stroking units, which he loved just as much. Which didn't mean that he gave up trying, he just was not as successful with it anymore.

So SPORT was his old self again. He gave us much pleasure with his antics and mischievous ways. He was nosy and curious just as before. He wanted to be part of everything and we included him in everything, we were just one happy pack. Over time, though – we hardly noticed it at first –

he did his walks at a somewhat more leisurely pace. And he also wanted to cut his outings shorter than before. Yes, SPORT was slowly becoming a senior. Occasionally, he still tried to chase a rabbit, but usually stopped after a few leaps, looking at George *"well, are you not going to go after it for me?"* No, George did not feel like chasing rabbits, so SPORT just resigned to watching them, probably dreaming of those hunting joys in his early years.

Now, where SPORT was becoming more aged, he began to avoid some of our old walking areas. There we usually ran into all the other dogs and their owners. Some of these dogs were still young and very playful and also wanted to include SPORT in their pranks. But when they jumped at SPORT or tried to put their paws on his back, SPORT sometimes lost his balance and fell over. This was really embarrassing for him. He resented this deeply and he began to growl at some of the really bold youngsters. As in many older dogs, SPORT's hind legs had become a bit weak and he had a harder time keeping his balance, especially in such roughhousing situations. So we began to go on different excursions where he would not be bullied by other younger and stronger dogs.

In his later years, SPORT developed a cough without having a cold. It really worried us. The vet explained to us that SPORT's heart had become weak and did not pump strong enough anymore, therefore water was retaining in his lungs, which caused the coughing, not uncommon in older dogs. This condition became more serious over time despite the stronger heart medication that SPORT received now. A short time before Christmas that year, the vet carefully indicated to us that it was advisable to get familiar with the thought of what to do when SPORT could not go on any more. We had feared this situation to come, but knew that it was unavoidable. For the time being, SPORT was given an injection to boost his energy and well-being. And during the following months, he was doing fine.

Then came the time again when it was necessary to carry SPORT up or down our stairs. We had noticed that he sometimes kind of stumbled, fell and then slid down the stairs on his belly. It seemed not to be just clumsiness, it looked more like weakness. He was not strong enough to get up again on his own and we had to pick him up. Walking up the stairs became also harder and harder for him to master. So we did as in his early puppy time, we picked him up and carried him again. He fought this in the beginning and mildly growled at us, as he still wanted to do it all by himself. He had his own hard head, wanted to be independent, be his own man. But eventually he realized that being carried was the best way without getting hurt.

It became obvious that SPORT now began to seek more body contact with us. He took his time to snuggle and be rubbed and stroked and cuddled. He loved these sessions more than ever. It seemed as if he needed an extra portion of reassurance. And we gave him all the love we could.

During the time just before the Easter holidays, SPORT became weaker again, he hardly wanted to go on his beloved walks anymore. Sometimes he stopped on the way, looking at us with fervent eyes "*come, let's go home again, I am tired*". It was heartbreaking to watch him this way. Everything appeared to have become too difficult and strenuous for SPORT to master. He really looked fatigued and tired, it seemed as if he did not have the will to go on anymore.

George and I discussed what to do and decided to go to the vet the following morning and let her take a look at him. It turned out to be one of the hardest and saddest things we ever had to do. Inside we knew that this might possibly be SPORT's last walk, but were still hoping that perhaps a treatment like the one he got just before last Christmas would postpone the unavoidable. When we arrived at the vet's and she saw SPORT, her sorrowful look was telling us that the time had now come. SPORT was resting on the floor, apathetic and too tired to get up by himself. We did not want to leave him behind alone with the vet and desert him at a time like this and so carried him into the doctor's office. And while holding him tenderly in our arms, the vet had him sliding softly into a deep sleep, before giving him the final injection to grant him eternal rest. While we were burying our faces in his fur for a long last time, saying good-bye, we were crying like little babies, including the vet and her assistant.

We were devastated, not speaking one word on our way home. Our beloved SPORT was gone, our devoted companion was not any more. Life seemed so unbearably empty. We knew before that we would not be able to think rational at this final moment, therefore we had already arranged earlier that SPORT should be cremated and his ashes sent back to us in an urn.

The following week we were very tense, waiting for the urn to arrive. When this finally happened, it was almost like a relief. The world once again began to look brighter to us, as SPORT was back home again, with his pack and where he belonged!

******

SPORT, we will miss you forever! Your spunk and friskiness, your never ending trust and loyalty, your natural dignity and your pride, your big tender and sensitive soul, your smartness and your sturdy and rugged good looks, your funny sides and your pure companionship. You have been everything to us that one could wish from a best friend, from a buddy, a comrade, and a companion. Yes, we are sad that you are gone, but we are also forever thankful that you were here and could be with us for all those years to share your life with us. You were a great SPORT and you will live on in our hearts until the end of time!

******

About the Author

Dorothee DeBerry, born 1942, lives in Frankfurt, Germany. After 45 years of work as secretary in advertising and logistics, she is now enjoying her retirement. Beside her great passion for travel she loves to be creative with drawing, painting, making videos and now also started to try out her skills in writing. She just had to tell and share the story about how this little rascal "SPORT the Schnauzer" came into her life and went straight to her heart.